I0764437

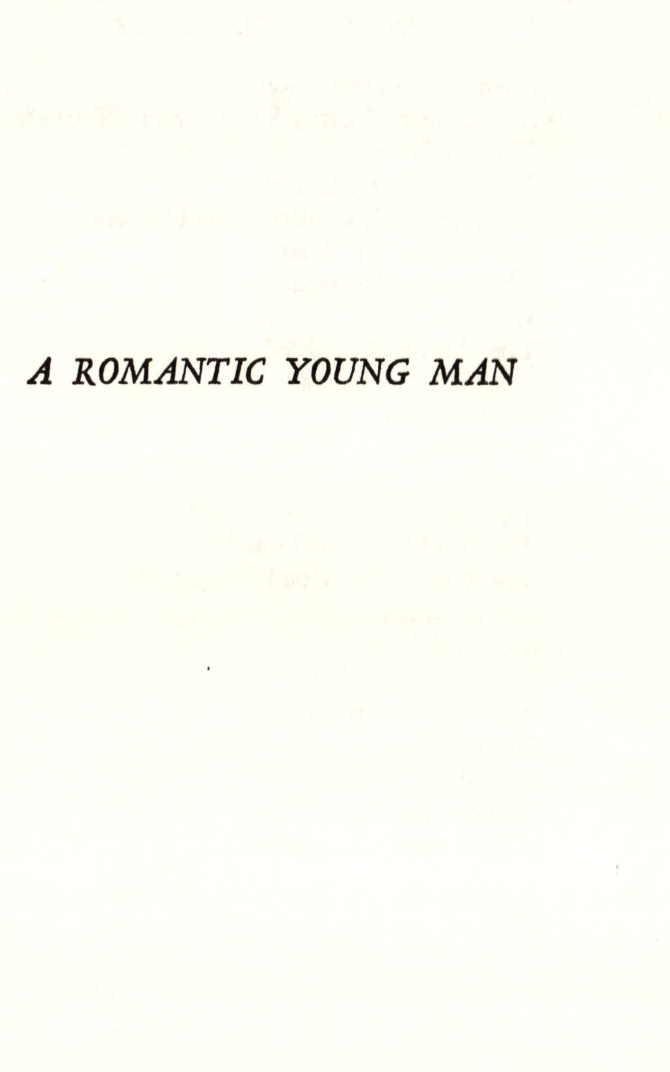

A ROMANTIC YOUNG MAN

BOOKS BY ACHMED ABDULLAH

Chansons Couleur Puce
A Grammar of Little Known Bantu Dialects
The Red Stain
The Blue-Eyed Manchu
The Honorable Gentleman and Others
The Trail of the Beast
The Man on Horseback
Wings
The Mating of the Blades
The Thief of Bagdad
Night Drums
Alien Souls
Shackled
The Swinging Caravan
The Wild Goose of Limerick
The Year of the Wood-Dragon
Ruth's Rebellion
Steel and Jade
They Were So Young
Broadway Interlude
Black Tents
The Veiled Woman
Girl on the Make
A Romantic Young Man

A ROMANTIC YOUNG MAN

by

ACHMED ABDULLAH

WILDSIDE PRESS

www.wildsidepress.com

PRINTED IN THE UNITED STATES OF AMERICA
BY THE FERRIS PRINTING COMPANY, NEW YORK

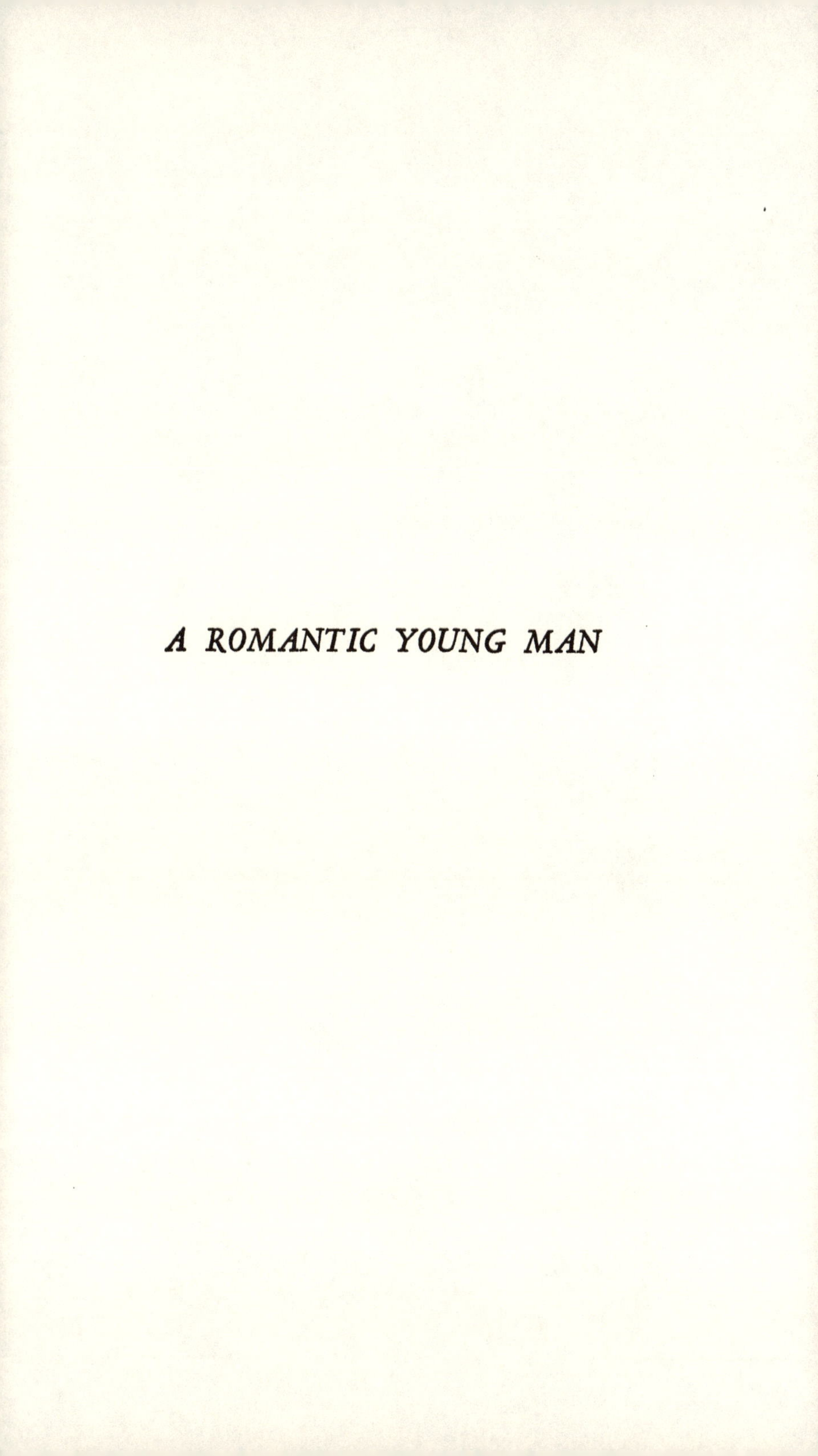

A ROMANTIC YOUNG MAN

CHAPTER ONE

GARTH BRENT was his name. Garth Van Rensselaer Brent. And, at least around Gramercy Park and Murray Hill, the Van Rensselaer part made a whole lot of difference.

For it proved that he was the descendant of a certain Dutch shipmaster who, early in the seventeenth century, had sailed out of Rotterdam, had fought his stout little, high-pooped sloop, armed with a single swivel brass cannon, against a gorgeous Spanish privateer that had mounted sixteen pieces, had rammed and beaten her, and had wound up the day's entertainment by hanging the surviving dons from their own yardarm, smoking his long churchwarden pipe the while and giving heartfelt, guttural thanks to his harsh Calvinistic God. It proved, by the same token, that he belonged to that Knickerbocker aristocracy which, in its aggressive, sardonically republican fashion, ranks itself with the Bourbons, the Hanovers, and the Hapsburgs, which patronizes mere Russian Grand Dukes and considers Balkan royalty decidedly parvenu and socially impossible.

He was thirty-two years of age; not bad-looking, rather short than tall, stocky and powerfully built, although graceful and with an unselfconscious ease in every gesture and movement that was almost Latin. Withal Garth Brent was intensely, tersely masculine; his round head covered thickly with close, light-brown curls; his mustache cropped army style; his nose strongly marked at the roots; his chin slightly prognathic; and his eyes sunk very deep, yet standing out, paradoxically, like signals.

There was in these eyes—which were of an extraordinary violet-blue—an expression that suggested a sort of reckless idealism. The active idealism of a doer, not the passive of a dreamer. The idealism of a man always ready to carry a stray leg of anybody's donkey. But it was contradicted by the ironic, downward curve to the mouth which seemed the result of over-sophistication . . . . "caused by women," according to his second cousin, the Vicomte Charles de Montfort, "too many women."

And perhaps the Frenchman was right. The other liked women—and they liked him.

Indeed he had a way with them. Nor was this way precisely hindered by his quixotic, romantic flair; his habit of falling in with, and playing up to, a woman's most histrionic and least sincere moods, of taking a woman—literally—at her face value.

Still, he did not often make a complete fool of himself—again thanks to his sophistication, his sudden realism in matters of the heart and the flesh. The heart and the flesh. Interchangeable terms, to him.

Thus, for instance, he did not hold with platonic friendship; had once been heard to remark that platonic friendship is shot to hell the moment the first baby arrives . . . . by which can be seen that his sense of humor was of that pungent, uniquely American brand so disturbing to Europeans.

His manner of living, on the other hand, was not American. Rather, it was more New York than strictly American, and more Park Avenue—with a dash of Westchester County and a suspicion of Piping Rock—than strictly New York. For he did nothing at all—and did it charmingly. So it was only natural that he should know all about handling a polo mallet and a rapier, a cocktail shaker, a deck of cards, a backgammon board, and a billiard cue.

He knew, furthermore, all about handling a golden mocha spoon and a Wedgwood tea cup with the right degree of nonchalance. But spoon and cup usually belonged to somebody else—since he was not rich.

During the world war he had done his bit. He had done it—to quote his own words—"in excellent taste and without the faintest trace of ostentation, of exhibitionism, I not having been in the marines."

By this sarcastic remark he did himself an injustice. He had fought bravely at the front, accumulating a baker's dozen of medals and ribbons. Later on, thanks to his familiarity with several languages, his shrewdness, and his keenly analytical mind, he had been transferred to the Military Intelligence Service and had done valuable work, being instrumental in bringing some notorious German spies before drum-head courtmartial and firing-squad. It had earned him a reputation; and, after peace had come, he had received a flattering offer to join the Diplomatic Secret Service —the service that, unknown to the daily press and the man in the street, makes and unmakes history.

But he had refused.

"No work for me!" he had decided.

And the place for no work was obviously Paris where he had been making his home now for a number of years. Not because he was a snobbish expatriate; the kind who speaks English with a French accent and French with an English, and who hates all countries, including his own. But because he found life abroad cheaper and not so hectic.

Besides, his parents were dead and he had a great many friends in France. Foremost amongst them was the Vicomte Charles de Montfort whose mother, née Emmeline Van Rensselaer, was related to him and who had been married, for over three decades, to the Duke de Montfort-Tonnerre, the type of booted, bewhiskered, rustic Norman nobleman who was more interested in pedigree cattle than in pedigree cocottes and who knew more about the proper sort of manure than the improper sort of mannequin.

The old duchess was built on the generous, broad-beamed lines of a Dutch frigate. Dutch, too, and reminiscent of her ancestors, the New Amsterdam padroons, was her quite amazing outspokenness.

Indeed she was very outspoken when, during a dinner-dance at her husband's Faubourg St. Germain palace, she turned on Garth—Garth who, for the last half hour or so, had been going from room to room; talking to the little Comtesse de Persignac, a deceptively appealing bit of femininity in wisteria charmeuse and copper lace; bowing before the parrot beak and shabby, rustling moire of an ancient Serene Highness; whispering into the pretty ear of a South American heiress who was trying to achieve Paris fame with the help of a string of three-carat, rose-pink diamonds; listening deferentially to the deep chest notes of a horsy lady of Yorkshire rectitude and angularity; parrying a resolute matron's challenge with a subdued buzz of mild expostulations; speaking to a dozen women and, in each case, vowing that he would attend to something which only he could do and which had to be done immediately.

Finally, rather exhausted, he had sunk down on a couch by the side of Charles de Montfort, and there the duchess had cornered him.

"Been attending to your regular business, haven't you?" she asked.

"My regular business . . . .?"

"Yes. Doing nothing."

"How you misjudge me, Aunt Emmeline. I've been doing all sorts of things . . . ."

"Useless things—for useless women. I know. You waste your life. You're a drone."

Garth looked discomfited; her son laughed; and she stared at the latter with disapproval.

"So are *you* a drone," she continued inexorably.

"I'm not, darling mother. I'm a most respectable government employee—squatting in the Bureau of Registry all day long—busy filling out little pink cards and little green cards and . . . ."

"And earning hardly enough money to buy orchids for whomever happens to be your mistress."

"My current mistress buys *me* orchids. She's frightfully emancipated and strong-minded . . . . believes in women's rights . . . ."

"Oh—be quiet, Charles!"

Again she addressed Garth.

"Why don't you work?" she demanded.

"Work?" he echoed. "How American you are—after a lifetime in Europe . . . ."

"And proud of it."

"Three cheers for the red, white and blue!"

"Please—be serious."

"All right. I'll be serious. How much money do you think I have?"

"The small fortune Aunt Caroline left you."

"Right. That—and no more. Invested in some New England factory. Brings me in five thousand dollars a year. Not much. And yet—I live well, don't I?"

"So it seems."

"And how—do you imagine—do I get away with it?"

"By making debts?"

"No. I work."

"Eh . . . .?"

"I work, I repeat."

"At what?"

"At useless things. Yes—to quote your own words—I do useless things for useless women. Take little Yvonne de Persignac, for instance. Saw me talk to her—didn't you, auntie?"

"Well . . . .?"

"She has written a perfectly wretched comedy that some society or other has performed for the benefit of the starving Eskimos or Armenians or Patagonians or what-have-you. And of course it was a success—and now she has a notion that she's a runner-up to Eugene O'Neill—and she has heard that George M. Cohan is coming to Paris next month—and she wants her play submitted to him. And who knows George? Who can get past his relays of secretaries? I! Result—George is going to take a squint at the title page of Yvonne's masterpiece. And further result . . . ."

"What?"

"I'm going to spend four lovely summer weeks at Yvonne's country place in Normandy. Four weeks' board and lodging—if you get what I mean."

"Oh . . . ."

"Same with the other women," Garth went on, and there was just the faintest trace of bitterness in his voice. "That South American heiress—the one with the diamond anchor chain—take her. Her pekinese has the pip or the flu or the d. t.'s or something—and I know all about who's fashionable and expensive among the hound surgeons. Result—tomorrow I play dry-nurse to a flat-nosed, soulless, snivelling pup—and that's good for a Mediterranean yacht cruise later in the year."

He paused; then continued:

"I'm the best-dressed man on the boulevards. That's a fact, isn't it?"

"I suppose so."

"How do I pay for it?"

"You don't."

"Wrong again. I do pay. Not in cash. Of course not. I pay by telling the young bucks round the Ritz lounge and the Cosmopolite Club smoking-room that so-and-so is my tailor and this-and-that my haberdasher and such-and-such my bootmaker and so on. In other words, I'm an American businessman. I capitalize my special gifts and . . . ."

"You are too impudent," interrupted the duchess in her rumbling basso profundo. "I know you. I've known you since you were a little tot. I've disapproved of you since that morning in Central Park—I recollect it perfectly—when you bit your governess in the ear because she insisted on your wearing long curls and talking French in public."

"But—you like me, darling?"

"I adore you. I am a woman—and weak."

"Weak? You?"

"Yes. In spite of my size."

She struck him smartly across the cheek with her old-fashioned, lace-and-ivory fan, while Garth and Charles smiled and stretched their legs comfortably and conversed pleasantly about this and that and the other thing: about Highflyer being a damned good mare to bet your roll on for the Grand Prix, and the new cocktail—half French vermouth and half apricot brandy—which Henri had invented over at the Ritz, and the Cannes polo matches, and the quite deplorable trick some people have of sprinkling their caviar with shredded onions, and how last week at the Cassagnacs the old Princess Natasha Demidova had dropped her false eyebrows into her soup plate and had chased them round and round with a spoon, thinking they were truffles.

They laughed. They usually laughed at the identical thing. This was one reason for their friendship. Another reason was the fact that—as Garth was in the habit of saying—they liked the same wines and different women; the woman who, most recently, had engaged the American's fancy being La Sylphe.

He spoke of her now. He spoke in that exaggerated, rather stilted manner which was a way of his—perhaps so as to hide his embarrassment under a cloak of self-ridicule—whenever he felt deeply moved; using phrases which he should not have used, since he was not a Montmartre poet with floppy, black sombrero, unkempt beard, and doubtful lingerie, but a sane young New Yorker whose perfectly fitting evening clothes had been cut by Mr. Poole and whose dancing pumps had been bench-made by M. Coquillot himself.

"Upon my honor—" he exclaimed—"for the sake of that girl I would do anything. Deeds I would do—fabulous and storied deeds!"

"You aren't drunk—by any chance?"

"I've been on the wagon for a week. My liver, you know—and that lousy gin—must have imported it from America—we had at the Regniers' shin-dig . . . ."

"Then you are mad, my dear fellow. As mad as all Yankees. Her figure is lovely—I grant you. But her face . . . ."

"Is lovely, too. I'm sure of it."

"Don't be an ass! You haven't the faintest notion what she looks like."

It was the truth. Garth did not know what La Sylphe looked like. Nor did anybody else in Paris.

She was a dancer who had come to the Ambassadeurs a few months earlier; who, from the night of her first appearance, within a minute of her lithe, young body swaying out of the wings in a tumbled cloud of purple and silver draperies, had become a sensation.

She had remained a sensation. And it had been accentuated by the fact that nobody had ever seen her away from the stage without a thick veil covering her features, while, during the performance, she wore a stark, painted Javanese mask.

The reason . . . .?

"Publicity stunt," some said.

Others claimed that she was hiding a disfiguring scar. Still others insisted that she belonged to a noble, proud, impoverished family which was ashamed of her profession.

At all events, she was a tremendous success. Paris was at her feet. Paris accepted her as a great artist—and a great mystery. And Paris dotes on its mysteries and included her, presently, amongst the other mysteries which have become part of the city's contemporary annals: like the tall, white-bearded Highland Scot who, every afternoon, walks from the Porte St. Martin to the Arc de Triomphe, dressed in kilt and plaid, horn-handled dagger in stocking, sporran swinging rhythmically from side to side, and followed by a piper playing "Lochiel's awa' to France" on the droning, skirling, full-throated war-pipes; like the blind American who twice a week, rain or shine, takes his seat on the pavement outside of the Café de Naples and distributes gold pieces to all passers-by; like the plum-colored, tattooed Senegalese who, every morning promptly at five, prays in front of Napoleon's tomb, his hands spread out like the sticks of a fan, his huge, round, frizzy head bobbing up and down with the fervor of his savage, jungly incantations.

Nor did the fact that, for whatever reasons, she hid her features beneath veil or mask, lessen the desire of man. And so there seldom passed a day that did not bring her a decent proposal of marriage or less decent proposal of strictly temporary alliance from aristocrat or rich bourgeois, from anemic, white-collared clerk or blue-bloused workman or dreamy, long-haired Montparnasse artist; never a night that did not see brass-buttoned messengers arrive at the stage door of the Ambassadeurs with jewels and flowers—the jewels to be sent back to the donors, the flowers to go to some hospital—until, toward the end of the season, to say on the boulevards "when La Sylphe loses her heart" was synonymous with saying "when Monday falls on Tuesday . . . ."

Garth lit a cigarette.

"Charles," he declared, "I've been thinking about her."

"About whom?"

"La Sylphe. Who else?"

"Oh . . . ." The Frenchman was impatient.

"I've been thinking that she's the sort of woman who should always dress in white—simple, glorious, amazing white—and a necklace of seventy black pearls around her throat, with a clasp made of a single blue diamond—and . . . ."

"And cigarettes wrapped in rose leaves," cut in the other, "and an emerald-green jade bowl for an ash-tray. I know the patter." He smiled. "What a charming lover you would be—if you had a million francs a year."

"Don't be absurd! I could spend that much on orchids for her narrow feet to step on."

"What a fool you are! What a sentimental Anglo-Saxon fool!"

"Say—" and Garth's language was no longer romantic—"let me tell you what I think about *you*, you miserable little, frog-eating . . . ."

They laughed. They insulted each other freely. It was a way they had.

For they were the best of pals and usually managed to spend twelve hours out of the twenty-four in one another's company. They went about together not only in the exclusively French milieu of the Faubourg St. Germain, but also in the rather more English and American milieu of the Ritz bar, and in the entirely cosmopolitan milieu of the Paris underworld where they slummed as a New Yorker does in Harlem, or a Californian in Florida—or vice versa.

This was not the drab underworld of former years that had coiled and moiled and stewed and smelled to high heaven in the neighborhood of the rue de Venise; the underworld of the traditional, almost legendary Apache with peaked cap, waspish waist, pointed, yellow shoes, and homicidal longings. But it was a new underworld—more polite and quite as dangerous as the old—that had evolved when Paris, at the end of the war, had become a haven for the once great, the now down-and-out. A perfumed, silk-stockinged, monocled underworld it was—with a flavor of disgraced Russian Grand Dukes, an aroma of deposed Balkan princelings, a taint of degenerate Austrian aristocrats who had passed through the three p's of life: from prince to pauper, and from pauper to pimp.

These people had exchanged the sacred hostage of their mutual degradation. They were linked by a chain stronger than friendship or kinship, since it had been tempered by misery and tested by shame. So, even in adversity, they were clannish. They obeyed the herding instinct of their class. They had their own restaurants, their own bawdy-houses, their own clubs.

One of the latter was in the rue de Turbigo. It was called "*Le Cercle des Ratés*", the Club of the Failures.

Named so rightly, with bitter, grimacing self-irony, it being a club—precisely—for men who had failed.

They were well-bred, mostly titled failures. Failures not always due to their own fault. For, though some of them were youths tossed about by every wind of adventure and self-indulgence, incapable of any discipline except that of dressing for dinner and differentiating between a salad fork and an ice-cream fork, others were the victims of circumstance. They were the victims of that world revolution which, following upon the Versailles treaty, had stalked through Europe—upsetting thrones, upsetting historic fortunes, upsetting éthical and civilizational values, substituting new values, creating new millionaires, and leaving only the vices intact.

The club was in need of money. So, in the evenings, it threw open its doors to paying guests. Not very successfully at first. Paris was too blasé to prefer an atmosphere of spurious romance and second-hand coronets to clean comfort and a decent cuisine.

Then, all at once, a few months earlier, thanks to the murder there of a famous Hungarian nobleman by an equally famous Hungarian communist, the club had become the fad and fashion. It had become, sardonically, through red tragedy, the center of all that bizarre Paris night life where real society mingles with parvenus, foreigners, artists, professional and amateur cocottes. Night after night Paris had foregathered there; to dine and dance and flirt and get drunk; to buy bad champagne at three hundred francs a bottle and Californian grapes at five hundred francs a small basket; to parade its arrogant luxury of furs, pearls, diamonds, and naked flesh; to glory in brazen licentiousness, in money thrown out of windows, in excessive and discordant noises, in crude frankness of word and gesture, in a very orgy of public neurosis—the neurosis which was the symbol of post-war Europe, of the new freedom, the triumph of life and lust over death; perhaps the right medicine for these people whom the war had decimated and crushed and enervated, for the two sexes who, during five years, had been separated by a wall of earth and mud and iron and fire, and who now once more had found each other, orgastically starved, anxious to meet, to kiss and embrace and mate.

Yes. The war, that supreme moratorium of human will and human liberty, had ceased to function. Again men were responsible to themselves—and irresponsible to others; were singing the paean of the living, instead of ringing the tocsin and toll for the dead . . . .

The Club of the Failures had reaped its share of popularity and gold. But not for long.

Quickly, as always, Paris had transferred its fickle affections elsewhere. This time to a Montmartre cabaret where, for the mere pittance of a hundred francs, any woman, decent or courtezan, could dance with a six-foot, odorous Central African negro, guaranteed by a truthful management to be a cannibal—while, again, the club had sunk into the slough of neglect and penury.

Yet it was still under discreet police surveillance and political suspicion. It was still mentioned occasionally; not only by silly old women bargain-hunting for titled, tangoing gigolos, but also by grave and proper gentlemen of substance . . . . as for instance tonight, in the palace of the Duke de Montfort-

Tonnerre, where important French officials jostled foreign diplomats, where grand seigneurs from Normandy and the Auvergne, mortgage-ridden and eager for market tips, buttonholed bankers of international renown, and where one of the latter suggested that, for the sake of Europe's peace and the security of Wall Street and the Paris *bourse*, the club should be blown sky-high with dynamite.

"Rather radical procedure, don't you think?" smiled Garth who, with Charles, had joined the group.

"Not radical enough, considering that most of the members are from Wallachia . . . ."

"And royalists . . . ."

"Royalists," added a Chicago financier, a man of a teasing, freckled turn of mind, quite out of keeping with his solid millions and his solid fame, "are no longer the fashion. That's one thing my native land has done for civilization and progress."

"Tell me," mocked Henri Duteil, the editor of a great Paris daily, "didn't your oldest daughter marry a king?"

"A former king, my dear Henri. I saw to his reform. He now addresses envelopes and licks stamps in my London office—and seems a very happy young man."

"I wish you'd give a similar job to Prince Danielo of Wallachia."

"Is he making trouble?"

"Not yet. But God knows what'll happen when he comes of age—a week from Saturday."

"Zero hour—eh?"

"Yes. And perhaps another Armageddon—another world war. . . ."

The talk became general. A certain nervousness was in the air; a certain tension; a certain fear.

These last few days, the newspapers had been filled with rumors and speculations about Wallachia, the semi-barbarous, semi-Oriental country at the back door of South-Eastern Europe, pinched in between Roumania and Turkey, which, ever since the end of the world war, had run a most bloody gamut of civic strife. There had been revolution by the Reds and temporary success, with King Mirko forced to flee; White counter-revolution; the king reinstated, then murdered; and on the eve of his coronation—suddenly, dramatically, for reasons never made public—the abdication of Crown Prince Karolus who had left Wallachia immediately afterwards with his younger brother, Danielo, and the latter's twin-sister, Nadine.

Finally a republic had been founded. But it was not very stable. There was frequent turmoil, with Reds as well as Whites, both enemies of the established government, continuing their intrigues.

Thus, once more, as so often in the past, the land was about to become the cock-pit of Europe. It was anxiously watched by the war-weary Western nations; doubly watched today, with Danielo's approaching coming of age, with nobody able to foretell if he would claim the throne and plunge Wallachia into another orgy of bloodshed, or if he would follow Karolus' example and renounce his rights to succession.

For the young prince had disappeared—as Nadine had disappeared.

"This disappearing stunt runs in the family," observed the newspaper editor. "I remember years ago—when the late king's twin-brother. . . ."

"Oh—" inquired the duchess—"did he have a twin, too?"

"Yes. That's another thing that runs in the family."

"Wasn't his name Breda?"

"That's it. And he vanished. . . ."

"Was forced to vanish, you mean."

"Why?"

"He was a mad, passionate, hot-headed youngster. Was in love with an actress. The king tried to interfere—and Breda grew furious, took the bit between his teeth, shouted from the roof tops that he had as much right to the throne as his brother, made a tremendous row, and—well—there was a convenient monastery with exceedingly stout walls, and the cunning little official tale that Breda had got religion and would hereafter live a life of pious devotion."

"Is he dead?"

"Shouldn't wonder. The monastery was destroyed during the war. . . ."

"Bombed by Russian airplanes."

"But suppose," suggested Garth, "he should turn up alive and very much kicking . . . .?"

"And make a bid for throne and sceptre? Not a chance. He would not be able to stir up enthusiasm and find adherents. You see—a pretender must always be young and handsome—like Bonnie Prince Charlie. . . ."

"Danielo is handsome enough—I've seen him. . . ."

"If he'd only show up," said a French cabinet minister, "and declare his hand—one way or the other. Waiting for a revolution is more dangerous and nerve-racking than the revolution itself."

"I do not approve of revolutions," exclaimed a Swedish baroness, a née Miss Levy, adjusting her gold-rimmed monocle. "Some day they'll spell the end of royalty, of aristocracy."

"Royalty? Aristocracy?" jeered the newspaper editor who remembered at incongrous moments that he was a republican whose grandfather had fought and died behind the street barricades of the Paris Commune. "What are they? Intellectually? Negative! Morally? Degenerate! Spiritually? Turgid! Financially . . . .?"

"Bankrupt!" interrupted a Spanish grandee who, recently, had settled with his creditors for seven centimes in the franc, while a noble British earl chimed in, giving a cruel caricature of his own, exaggeratedly Norman features:

"And physically—why—we're mostly a breed with processional noses and recessional chins!"

Then there was laughter. There was, at once, a shimmering, vying exchange of repartee, shifting quickly from the political to the personal, from the general to the intimate; a twisting of phrases and epigrams that were intemperately, preposterously clever; a making and unmaking of reputations good or bad for the sake of a *bon mot;* men and women buffeting the air with pinchbeck, verbal thunder, ripping it with counterfeit, electroplated lightning; suavely accomplishing metaphorical rape and reveling in philosophical catharsis; saying things they hoped would be thought brilliant and quoted—with due credit given—or be thought profound and meditated over.

Garth listened. He felt faintly annoyed.

In his way, he was a typical American. Not the American of the little red schoolhouse and the little white church, of goatee and clam-chowder and spelling-bee and icecream-social. But the American of the roaring, bragging, gigantic Twentieth Century who, architecturally and psychologically, piled skyscraper upon skyscraper, who invented machines to regulate machines and multiplied speed by speed. An American of that mad, incredible New York—or it might have been Chicago or Cleveland or San Francisco—that was like Babylon mated to a three-ring circus. Thus—logically—an American of the wise-cracking era.

He liked wise-cracks. They expressed to him—something. Something quite important. Something in himself. Too, something of the age to which he belonged. They were modern, sharp, crackling. They were in tune with the up-to-date, jazzy symphony. Coined on the spur of the moment, they gave—rather cynically—the spirit of that same moment.

But these epigrams he was listening to . . . .? These bits of repartee . . . .? They were so carefully cut to measure, so deliberate, so artificial, so self-conscious. Begging for applause they seemed; for cries of "Author! Author!"

They bored him—as the whole party was beginning to bore him.

He turned to Charles de Montfort.

"Let's beat it," he whispered.

"I'm willing."

"What about taking in the midnight show at the Ambassadeurs?"

"And giving La Sylphe a hand . . . .? Not for me. I've seen enough of her. Three times last week—twice the week before. . . ."

"Well—what'll we do? It's too early for bed."

"Suppose we drop in at the Cosmopolite?"

"Good idea," agreed Garth. "They 'phoned me this afternoon. Seems they've a cable for me. . . ."

"Perhaps your Uncle Cornelius died and left you a pot of money."

"I could use it. I need a car."

"All right. Let's go and find out."

CHAPTER TWO

THE Cosmopolite was their club. Garth had lived there until a few months ago when, with his colored servant, he had taken an apartment near the Place de Fontenoy where rents were cheap. Some of his American mail still reached him at the former address.

Housed in an immense, gray, medieval stone pile, it was a famous club—quite different from the Club of the Failures—where, if you were rich enough or of sufficient social importance, you could play any game of chance you fancied for any stake that you could, or perhaps could not, afford; where you could bet on the weather, on the number of times the Prince of Wales would fall from his horse during the coming hunting season, and on your belief or doubt that a Catalan patriot would murder King Alfonso before the end of the year. Or, if you preferred, you could catch yourself a certain eccentric Scotch duke and lay him long odds that the first fly that buzzed through the window would light on his nose, and not on yours—or the other way around.

Some of the card sessions there had passed into the annals of Paris as historic events.

For instance an evening of contract bridge for five hundred dollars a point, in which two English steel magnates had matched their skill, not to mention their smoldering business antagonism, against two American steel magnates. A round of piquet where one man had wagered his entire fortune and his opponent no more nor less than a package of love letters, yellow and brittle and dusty with age. A two-handed game of stud-poker in which Sir Isaac Oppenheimer, that recently ennobled British-South African financier, had lost his claim to Mademoiselle Odette Frescaly of the Folies Marigny to a Chicago magazine editor on the turn of an ace.

A club it was whose members ranged all the way from the Peerage of France to the Beerage of England, from Pekin to Paducah, and from the Almanac de Gotha to the Almanac de Ghetto.

Queer people, some of them.

And amongst the queerest was Sir Pascal Nahadin —a man with a nondescript Balkan name, a British title, an Italian mistress, a Russian passport marked "strictly temporary," and complete command over a dozen languages; an old man, incredibly, fantastically wealthy; a man of a most amazing culture who seemed to have read everything and to know everything, from primitive Chinese art to the home policy of the ancient Peruvians, from St. Thomas Aquinas to Dionysius of Halicarnassus; a man, finally, of no nationality that anybody had ever been able to discover and about whose past very little, indeed practically nothing, was known.

At the crucial height of the world war, a year before the United States had joined the fray and made an end of it, he had appeared, rather vaguely, out of the nowhere. He had taken an immediate spotlight on the financial and political stage of Paris by investing millions in French and British war loans, at a time when the Allied Powers were on the verge of bankruptcy and military defeat, with the Germans making their greatest effort to break the western front and Paris shivering in its boots, listening to the immense roar of the artillery salvos that sounded like a giant beating a huge drum and seeing the far sky swallowed in an intolerable peacock-blue, nicked with livid purple.

Of course, shortly after his arrival, he had been interviewed by a high official of the French Secret Service who had bluntly demanded:

"Who are you?"

The other had produced his passport; and the Frenchman had smiled thinly, had added:

"Temporary passport. Therefore meaningless. Too, it might be forged."

"Why don't you communicate with Moscow—and find out particulars?"

"Moscow, as you know, is in a turmoil."

"That's right."

"So—I repeat—who are you?"

"A multimillionaire who is investing largely in your war loans—and who, if you bother him too much, might become bored and . . . ."

"And . . . .?"

"Germany, too, has bonds for sale."

"A threat?"

"And a promise. Curb your curiosity about me—I assure you, incidentally, that I am a gentleman and a man of honor—and I shall keep on putting my resources at the disposal of your government."

"Your resources are unlimited?"

"No. But big enough to influence—a little—the course of history."

So a sort of bargain had been struck. Hereafter, at least officially, the French Secret Service operatives had left Pascal Nahadin alone. If, unofficially, they had discovered his identity—the which is a moot point—they had not broadcast the news.

He, on the other hand, had continued investing enormously in the war loans of the Allied Powers, thus proving himself a friend in need. Thence, presently, the distinctions which had been heaped upon his head: the British knighthood, the *grand cordon* of the Legion of Honor, the entree into every proper house in the Mayfair and on the Faubourg St. Germain. Thence, too, in spite of his age and his Italian mistress, more than one matron with spinster daughter of certain, or uncertain, age preparing a marital trap with the help of charming little, intimate dinners, decent vintage champagne, and daughter's virginal bosom chastely exposed to Sir Pascal's ironic monocle. . . . Sir Pascal who would look his fill, eat his fill, drink his fill, and then return to his mistress and his millions which, since the war, he had vastly increased.

For his was the Midas touch. His fortune beggared the Rothschilds'. It dwarfed the Vanderbilts'. It topped Henry Ford's.

Not that he hoarded his money. He was generous. He gave freely to charity.

Yet the questions persisted:

"How did he get his start?"

"Who is he?"

"What is his real name?"

And, as answers to these questions, would come grim, mysterious, exotic tales. Tales that were whispered and, usually, gave the lie to each other.

Thus, for instance, one man declared he had authentic proof that Sir Pascal was a German aristocrat who, decades ago, had been kicked out of the army for cheating at cards and who had drifted to West Africa where he had become a slaver, a dealer in "black ivory," raiding the Congo as far as Comba and Brazzaville. Another asserted, with equal positiveness, that once Sir Pascal had been a Russian nihilist, a Siberian convict who had discovered the buried treasure of Genghiz Khan, the Mongol conqueror, in the neighborhood of Lake Baikal, and had made his escape. Still another insisted that Sir Pascal was originally a Turkish Jew who had sold his soul to the Devil for the alchemists' secret of turning base metal into gold. It was typical of post-war Paris—typical of the hysterical wave of mysticism that was sweeping over the boulevards, bringing the thrill and, perhaps, the comfort of astrology, of numerology, of crystal-gazing, of mediums that sent psychic messages and sent them mostly "collect"—that even the third tale found devout believers.

There were many other tales. Often mere hints, half-tones, allusions.

All fantastic. Nearly always contradictory.

And it was Garth Brent who had once made the shrewd guess that Sir Pascal himself was inventing and spreading most of them the better to muddy his trail—for whatever cause.

This man of mystery was sitting in a corner of the small, yellow salon of the Cosmopolite, adjacent to the main card room, as Garth and Charles entered. Nobody else was in the room. The three exchanged polite, rather formal bows. Their acquaintanceship was slight.

"The cable that came for you—" Charles reminded his friend.

"Oh yes."

The American called a servant who left and returned a few minutes later. He brought, not one telegram, but two. He gave the first to Garth, the second to Sir Pascal who opened the blue envelope and read the contents; and the former, happening to look up, noticed that the financier had grown pale, that his hands shook violently, that an expression of fear and horror was crinkling his lean, brown features.

He was about to bring it to the attention of the Frenchman who had picked up a late evening paper and was scanning the headlines. But, for no reason except a subconscious one, he refrained. He opened and read his own telegram. And, the next moment, he almost duplicated Sir Pascal's behavior.

He, too, grew pale. His hands trembled. His lower jaw sagged.

He exclaimed:

"Oh . . . ."

"What's up?" asked Charles. "Was I right? Did Uncle Cornelius cash in his earthly checks?"

"On the contrary."

"On the contrary . . . .?"

"Yes. You see—" Garth's laugh was forced—"it's *my* earthly checks that are bothering me—and the fact that I shall *not* be able to cash them hereafter."

"Meaning . . . .?"

"That I'm broke—stony-broke."

"You're jesting."

"I wish to God I were. Heard me mention that New England concern in which my small capital is invested?"

"Well . . . .?"

"It has gone the way of all flesh—and many corporations. Up the spout, in other words. Bankrupt."

"Oh—it can't be."

"It is. All over—but the shouting."

"What are you going to do?"

"Haven't the faintest notion."

"Of course—look here, Garth—you're welcome to everything I have . . . ."

"I know, old man. And I'm grateful. Nor am I proud. I wouldn't mind sponging on you till the cows come home. But you haven't much yourself—with your father holding the purse strings . . . ."

"And my mother bullying my father into playing the stern parent. That's true." Charles was silent; then continued: "I've an idea."

"Spill it."

"Marry rich. Yvonne de Persignac, for instance. She has lots of money—and is keen on you."

"I don't happen to be keen on her."

"All right—if you must be picky and choosy—what about the little Bischoffsheim girl? Her father is a banker—and you like her . . . ."

"I don't like her—that way. Besides, aren't you forgetting that I'm in love?"

"With that dancer?"

"Yes."

"The more reason why you must marry money."

"I fail to see . . . ."

"Dancers are expensive. How else—unless you marry money can you afford to keep her?"

"Quite the cynical little oh là là Frenchman, aren't you?"

"I'm giving you good advice."

"I don't doubt it. Only—I really love the girl. I'll marry her some day."

"Good God!"

"I mean it."

"Suppose you do—what'll you live on? Being such a noble, moral Anglo-Saxon all of a sudden—though, in the past, I've known you to pipe a different tune—you can't possibly live on what she earns, can you?"

"Nor do I intend to. Perhaps your mother was right. Honest work may have the thrill of novelty."

"You're not fit for honest work."

"Is that so?"

"You bet that's so. You know all the charming things—and not a single useful one."

"Never mind. Let's talk of something else." Garth lit a cigarette. "Any news in the paper?"

"The usual rigamarole. Seventeen gentlemen with checked suits and no foreheads put on the spot in your native country. England extending the dole to her entire population so that in the future no free-born Briton will have to work. Einstein proving the infiniteness of the infinite . . . ."

"And somebody else inventing the noiseless soup spoon?"

"Shouldn't wonder," laughed Charles. "And, of course, more rumors from Wallachia. Talk that the Whites have got a hold of Prince Danielo who will claim the throne. And something about an airplane accident . . . ."

"Oh—where . . . .?"

"Near Lyons. Big Fokker crashed down. The pilot killed. The passenger—there was only one—badly injured."

"Someone we know?"

"His identity hasn't been established yet."

They smoked for a while in silence. Then Charles yawned and rose.

"Coming?" he asked.

"No. I want to do a little thinking."

"Well—don't worry. Everything will straighten out."

He left; and, a moment later, having first carefully closed both doors, Sir Pascal Nahadin approached the young American.

His words were short, clipped, direct:

"So you're broke—eh?"

"Been eavesdropping?" smiled Garth.

"Yes," was the calm admission. "That's one way of getting important information."

"Mean to say that the deplorable state of my finances is of importance to you?"

"Indeed—combined with the other things I know about you."

"Such as . . . .?"

"That you're a gentleman—and of a rather quixotic turn of mind—and inclined to be reckless . . . ."

"And somewhat of a fool . . . .?"

"Since you say it yourself . . . ."

"Thanks for the buggy ride!"

"Besides, I happen to know that you're amongst the three finest swordsmen in France."

Garth was not ill-pleased.

"No use denying it," he replied.

For it was a fact. His fame, when it came to the handling of naked steel, was solidly based. It had earned him Paris' admiration and envy; had been responsible, too, for quite a little amusement and laughter, his duels—there had been more than a few—being at times extravagant as to cause.

Once, for instance, he had crossed rapiers with the Marquis de Tourcoing-Cassagnac, a notorious Gasçon bully, because the latter, in the American's own words, had had "the effrontery to eat tripe at a table next to mine—tripe *with* garlic, my dear sir!"

And, recently, there had been the affair with Major Kostitch, the Bulgarian statesman who, come to France on a diplomatic mission, had made a quite undiplomatic and unfriendly remark about the United States; had later on related, in his naif Slav way, that his wife, mistrusting the Paris temptations, had ordered him to return speedily and, to make assurance doubly sure, had packed only one clean shirt in his trunk.

"But," Garth had exclaimed, "isn't that a futile precaution, given your nationality?"

And so, the following day, he had taken the Bulgarian out and had wounded him painfully in the arm, afterwards making ironic amends by sending him a dozen of his own shirts.

Sir Pascal laughed reminiscently.

"Poor Major Kostitch!" he said; and added: "Your courage is like your sense of humor—superb."

"Again—thanks for the buggy ride! But I had an idea that mere physical courage is at a discount these days—like—oh—belief in God . . . ."

"You're wrong on both counts. Courage still matters. So does religion."

There was a pause. Then Sir Pascal asked:

"And so—you wish to earn your living?"

"Wish? Don't be silly. I'd much prefer to have somebody else earn my living for me."

"But—there is no somebody else?"

"Exactly. Annoying—don't you think?"

"How much do you need?"

"What do you mean—how much do I need?"

"How much a year?"

"Five thousand will do me very nicely. Dollars, of course. Not francs."

"In other words, figuring at five per cent, if I should let you have one hundred thousand dollars capital . . . ."

"That's it," interrupted Garth with a laugh, thinking the whole thing a joke. "You may deposit the amount at the Paris branch of the National City Bank."

"I'll attend to it first thing in the morning."

Something in Sir Pascal's accent caused the younger man to look up sharply.

"Pulling my leg?" he inquired.

"Not at all."

"What's the idea? Not even millionaires hand out neat little fortunes without reason."

"Chiefly not millionaires. Or they wouldn't keep their millions."

"All right. Let's hear the dirt. What do you want me to do? Mayhem—arson—barratry—or plain murder?"

Sir Pascal was silent, while Garth stared at him. He was interested; was a little uneasy. For there was something eerie and menacing in the atmosphere, and he recalled the other's queer, vague reputation. Yet, somehow, he liked the man. Nor did he precisely mistrust him.

Besides, it seemed an adventure—an adventure to appeal to his romantic soul . . . .

"Well . . . .?" he went on. "Has it anything to do with the telegram you got a while back?"

Sir Pascal was startled.

"Oh—" he stammered—"you—you saw . . . .?"

"I saw your face. Not exactly a poker face—just then."

Sir Pascal inclined his head.

"You're right," he said. "It has something to do with the telegram." He leaned forward and lowered his voice. "I'll tell you what I want you to do. I want you to go to a certain place—and wait there for a certain thing to happen."

"What thing?"

"I don't know. Really—" he repeated, as Garth made an impatient gesture—"I don't know."

The other shrugged his shoulders.

"Very well—if you insist on being mysterious. Where am I supposed to go—and when?"

"Tonight. To the Club of the Failures. They're giving a masked costume ball. People without mask and costume not admitted. You must be there before two in the morning—and . . . ."

"And . . . .?"

"Wait for a girl."

"Just my meat. Is she pretty?"

"Who knows? You see—she never shows her face."

"Oh—" Garth made a quick guess—"La Sylphe is it—the dancer . . . .?"

"Yes."

"And—" the other was excited—"you want me to . . . .?"

"To help her. She may need your help."

"How?"

"Again—really—I don't know. You must watch

—use your own judgment—act as you think right. Will you do it?"

"A tall order. But try and stop me!"

Garth was delighted. La Sylphe—he thought—whom he wanted so to meet . . . .

"What about a costume?" he went on. "Where'll I get it? It's way past midnight."

"Come to my house. I have it all ready for you."

"I call that service," smiled the American, hiding his rising agitation beneath his flippancy.

They left the Cosmopolite. They drove through the purple night in the financier's Sunbeam car.

Garth was prey to conflicting emotions; the rational part of his brain clashing with the irrational; the rational arguing: "You're crazy! Don't rush helter-skelter into the unknown!" The irrational replying: "The unknown is always the glorious! Keep going!"

He turned to the older man:

"No use asking you to be less mysterious—and more explicit?"

"No use at all."

"Suppose I hadn't been at the club tonight—or had refused to fall in with your plan—whom would you have sent in my place?"

"I don't know."

"Wouldn't have gone yourself—eh?"

"No. I am old . . . ."

"Nor a fool—as I am . . . .?"

"I too, am a fool. That's why we like each other—we do, don't we?—because of this foolishness, this madness, which we have in common."

"My aunt Emmeline says that foolishness is a vice."

"She is mistaken. It is a virtue. The fool—to quote a Russian proverb—has God in his soul."

He stopped. They had arrived at Sir Pascal's house—a little marble palace, cool and white and gleaming, pagan in its Greek simplicity, whose charming exterior gave the lie to its sinister history.

For, forty years earlier, Prince Trachenberg-Donnersmarck, an immensely wealthy German aristocrat, had built it for that notorious and intemperately beautiful Polish cocotte, Fanya Vielomirskaya. Twelve months later, he had caught her in the arms of his younger brother. He had killed them both; had killed himself. Then Baron Sigismondo Doria, the Portuguese racing man, had purchased the property for Madame de Paiva whom he had won at baccarat from his maternal grandfather, the Duke de Braganza. She had ruined Doria with her fantastic, sadistic extravagances that had meant the continuous paying of blackmail to valets, maids, and the police; and again there had been murder and blackmail.

So people had become afraid of the house. For a long time it had stood empty.

Finally Sir Pascal had bought it. And, of course, croaking ravens of ill omen had been ready to lay odds that he would share the black fate of his predecessors.

But they had been doomed to disappointment. Sir Pascal's mistress, Signora Carlotta Cuneo, neither deceived nor ruined him. Instead, tenderly, she looked after him; tenderly looked after him tonight, when he entered and introduced Garth, when—a woman still soft of mouth and clear of eye, with the most wanton, chestnut curls and a graceful briskness of body that showed little sign of her accomplished years—she kissed him and said in her deep contralto voice:

"I'm glad you're home. I have been worrying."

"Nothing to worry about, dear."

"Nothing . . . .? Oh . . . ."

She gave a short laugh. And Garth thought that here, half spoken, bitterly restrained, was drama. He felt acutely embarrassed; felt that he was an interloper, trespassing upon hidden, proud, tragic lives.

Signora Cuneo seemed to have forgotten his presence. She clung to Sir Pascal—as if unwilling to let him go, afraid to lose him.

"I love you—" she whispered—"because you are great-hearted—foolishly great-hearted . . . ."

"Please . . . ."

"You can forgive, best beloved. I cannot."

She left. The two men stared at each other.

"I—" Sir Pascal murmured ineffectually—"I am sorry . . . ."

"Oh . . . ."

"An alien soul—"

There was a silence. Then he went to the door.

"Just a minute," he said. "I'll get you the costume."

He walked out of the room and returned, shortly afterwards, with a black velvet half-mask and the court regalia of a Wallachian nobleman, complete from round fur cap with jeweled aigrette to cherry-red, pleated, knee-length coat.

"Let's see if it will do," he suggested.

The American put on the costume. He grinned rather sheepishly.

"I feel silly," he said. "Like Adam with his first fig leaf."

"No reason," smiled the older man. "You look stunning."

He opened a small safe and took out a glittering decoration which he pinned on Garth's chest.

"The final touch of splendor?" asked the latter.

"Splendor—and authenticity. Of course I can count on your absolute discretion? I have your word of honor that you won't mention this to a soul?"

"Yes."

"Thank you."

"Why don't you take me into your confidence—tell me the whole story . . . .?"

"I cannot."

"Because you don't trust me?"

"If I didn't trust you, would I have asked your

help? But—I cannot tell you. Too much depends on it. The fate of . . . ."

"Of what . . . .?"

"I cannot say more."

Garth was faintly annoyed.

"Very well. Suit yourself." He pointed at the clothes which he had taken off. "What about these?"

"I'll send them to your apartment . . . ."

"19 Place de Fontenoy."

"I'll remember. And the check—depend on it—will be deposited at your bank in the morning. You have enough money in your pocket for tonight?"

"Plenty."

There was a short silence. Sir Pascal made the sign of the cross. Somehow the atmosphere seemed tragic to Garth. He put this feeling into words:

"I sense—oh—tragedy . . . ."

"Do you?"

"Yes. Tragedy—a conflict between right and wrong . . . ."

Sir Pascal shook his head.

"No," he said. "Tragedy is a conflict of right—and right . . . ."

And, half to himself, while the young American left the room, Sir Pascal repeated:

"Yes. A conflict of right—and right . . . ."

CHAPTER THREE

THE costume hidden by his long raglan, the fur cap under his arm, Garth Brent hailed a taxicab and had himself driven toward the rue de Turbigo—through the ancient quarter where the bigot Ravaillac had murdered Henri the Fourth, best and most just of the kings of France; where, for centuries, Paris had dumped the unshriven corpses of its paupers in huge, underground vaults; where, until the revolution, the "Bell Man of the Dead," in flapping, wide-brimmed, black hat and loose, red robe painted with death's-heads, had paraded at night, in times of cholera and plague, dangling an enormous bell and chanting:

> *"Réveillez-vous, gens qui dormez!*
> *Priez Dieu pour les trépassés!"*

Bitter, blood-stained old streets. Streets from whose gutters seemed to arise a scent and memory of the past—something grim and dramatic that struck a corresponding chord in the heart of the young American; something akin to fear.

He was too courageous a man to deny that this

fear existed. He wished that he might telephone to his friend Charles de Montfort and tell him:

"Hop into your car and join me."

But there was his promise to Sir Pascal: discretion and silence. He would have to play a lone hand.

So he reached No. 17—the Club of the Failures. A fairly large building, it assaulted the night, from behind closed windows, with a stab and flare of lemon lights and a sensuous, hiccoughy strain of jazz.

He adjusted his mask; put on the fur cap; stepped from the taxicab.

Up and down the rue de Turbigo a gendarme was pounding his beat. Sharply, suspiciously, he looked at Garth. Then, with ironic Gallic resignation, as if telling himself: "It isn't my duty to arrest *everybody* who comes here," he shrugged his shoulders and passed on his way.

Garth pushed open the door. He heard the rhythmic clop-clop-clop of the policeman's heavy boots gradually lessening and becoming a memory of sound. He heard, in the distance, a church bell tolling the half-hour, bronze-tongued, insistent, trying to warn him—the queer imagining came to him: "Turn back, you fool! Turn back!" And he was conscious of a sensation as though—with the clop-clop-clop disappearing, the tolling of the church bell disappearing—there disappeared, too, the safety and sanity of ordinary life . . . .

He crossed the threshold and found himself in an oblong, outer hall. He remembered it from former visits; remembered the mural paintings, in the modern Slav manner, of a procession of nude, overfed young women, in purple and canary-yellow, and with abnormally developed hands and feet.

Several men, evidently servants, lolled about, conversing in some purring, exotic language which he did not understand. They saw him, and one of them called out:

"Malik!"

The latter, short, swarthy, hook-nosed, came from behind the reception desk.

"May I have your ticket?" he asked, approaching Garth.

"Haven't got one. How much?"

"Two hundred francs."

"Here you are." The American paid.

"Check your overcoat?"

"Sure enough."

Garth removed his raglan. His costume came into view. The decoration caught the light from a chandelier and glittered. And, with his keen power of observation, Garth did not miss Malik's sudden, sharp intake of breath nor the amazed expression in the black, hooded eyes; eyes that stared at him, as if endeavoring to pierce the mask; eyes that, a moment later, became cloudy, shrewdly expressionless, while the man bowed deeply and said:

"Good evening, Monseigneur!"

Garth gave a start.

Monseigneur—he echoed in his mind—the form of address given to Continental royalty and to princes of the blood . . . .

Well—he continued in his thoughts—why not? Here, in the Club of the Failures, titles were as thick as pea soup. He remembered that, at the time of the murder there of the Hungarian aristocrat, when the spotlight of publicity had been turned on full, it had been reported in the newspapers how one member, who drove a taxicab, was in reality an Austrian Archduke, how a cabaret dancer was a scion of the House of Romanoff, and how a most unsavory gigolo happened to be the second son of the recently deposed king of Afghanistan.

Oh yes. There must be more than one Monseigneur belonging to this club.

On the other hand, Garth wore a face mask. How then—he wondered—had Malik, if mistakenly, guessed at his rank . . . .?

The next moment, he considered that it must be due to the decoration blazing on his chest. Perhaps it was one of those swanky and exclusive trinkets—a kind of imperial trade mark—given only to royalty, as was, in former years, the Black Eagle of Prussia and the Bourbons' Order of the Golden Fleece.

Sir Pascal had said something of the sort; had mentioned the decoration's "authenticity." Yes—Garth decided—that must be it . . . . and so he entered the ballroom, and was promptly disappointed.

For he had expected to see something, if not precisely thrilling or bloodcurdling or melodramatic, then at least out of the ordinary. And all he did see was a fancy dress party—nor did it differ from any other fancy dress party given any other night, or possibly that very night, in Chicago, London, or Rome.

For here the same paunchy gentleman with the Scotch kilts and the flat feet flashed the same off-color diamonds before the same South Sea cannibal queen. The same Paleolithic warrior was splitting a magnum of dry champagne with the same three flappers whose combined garb would not have made a fair-sized napkin. The same Spanish bull fighter made the same assignment with the same Madame Pompadour in the same dark corner. The same George Washington reproved history by having a row with the same Napoleon over the same Cleopatra. The same giddy grandmother advertised the fact that her legs were still slim with the help of the same spangled, salmon-pink tights. The same stray tourist from Kansas City, brought here by the same cocotte, was praying to the spirit of the Chamber of Commerce that his mask would not slip. The same stout matron in a Gretchen costume of baby-blue velvet that gave a bold glimpse of enormous, decidedly un-Gretchenlike breasts, was stalking the same banker who, even in a Harlequin's gay motley, carried a check book in his hip pocket.

The same electric blaze leaped about the same grotesque decorations. The same symphony of smells, a cloying jumble of patchouli and perspiration, of essence of rose and quintessence of subway, assailed the nostrils.

The same powdery film flew up from the waxed floor and settled lightly on hair and gown, as couples jerked in the negroid abandon of the same belching, braying, rowdy Charleston . . . . men and women dancing; pumice-whitened teeth standing out, skull-like and ghastly, against the crimson clefts of laughing, open mouths; jaws contracted into stark grimaces of lust and rapture; arms twined tightly about waists; hairy, coarse, male hands gliding from narrow shoulders to supple hips, then up to caress bare spines—while, upon a platform, just as in Chicago or Rome or London, seven negro musicians tossed their instruments in gleaming circles, swaying in their chairs, bobbing frantically up and down, playing jazz—stammering, syncopated, jungly, lascivious.

Jazz—thought Garth—Africa's sardonic gift to civilization, perhaps in exchange for the slaver's yoke and whiskey and tuberculosis! Africa's sensuous, obscene soul translated by the genius of a Russian Jew composer, who should have known better, and filtered via Tin Pan Alley across the Atlantic—to help along an Americanization begun by dry martinis, safety razors, modern plumbing, chewing gum, Woodrow Wilson, and Charlie Chaplin . . . .

The saxophones wailed, the clarinets squeaked, as Garth crossed the room toward a number of small tables that framed the dance floor. They were crowded with men and women who were shouting, laughing, flirting, drinking, getting drunk, pawing each other. The masks of several of the women had slipped; showing some faces that were young and pretty; showing, mostly, faces that, after hours in this atmosphere surcharged with the fumes of alcohol and tobacco, had lost the artificial bloom of youth, had become wilted, haggard, flabby.

Caricatures of women, now that midnight had passed and left its tell-tale, treacherous marks. Sorry flowers, painted and glued; and presently, with the help of lipstick and rouge, of powder puff and pocket mirror, being repainted and reglued.

One table was empty. Garth took it. He called a waiter and—with a few hundred francs still in his purse and the conviction that in the morning his bank account would be replenished—ordered a bottle of his favorite vintage, Chateau Yquem '79.

He sat there. He was conscious of a queer sensation of being just on the outside of a drama enacted quite near to him; a drama alien to him, yet in which, at a given moment, obeying a given cue, he would have to play a part.

So he was nervous, a little excited. But he enjoyed himself thoroughly, sipping the golden, flower-scented wine and watching the dancing couples—more and more people joining in the Charleston, until there was hardly space left to move and the men and women, unable to budge and step, remained stationary, only the shoulders and thighs shivering convulsively, as if in a delirium of the senses.

Garth had a notion that, though all wore masks that covered their features from forehead to upper lip, he could pick out the club members from among the guests; could pick them out by token of a certain air of distinction that had survived disgrace and poverty, a certain swing and carriage, heads erect, shoulders well thrown back, martial clicking of heels when bowing before a woman for the favor of a dance, curt, clipped sharpness of accent in their drifting talk, in German, Russian, Magyar, Wallachian . . . . the whole speaking eloquently, and rather pathetically, of years spent in crack Continental regiments: in the late Tsar's Chevalierski and Viborgski, in Hungarian Hussars of the Guard, in the "*Maikäfer*" battalions of Prussia's departed pomp and glory.

These men interested him. He studied them, watched them alertly, found out a few of their names, as they addressed each other with the stilted ceremony of their class. There was, for instance, a Count Varolath; a Colonel de Milenko; and a Prince Tomashin, a burly giant in the scarlet and blue of a Napoleonic grenadier, with a great, crimson scar, evidently the mark of an old sabre cut, slashing across his jaw.

All Wallachian names—Garth said to himself—

names that, until war and revolution, had spelled great fame, great wealth, historic achievements. He grew more and more interested—and he noticed that, as he was watching them, so were they watching him.

Chiefly Tomashin. Several times he seemed on the point of approaching the table. But he reconsidered. He stood there; continued staring at the American.

The latter felt more than saw that steady glance. He felt bitter venom in it, lust of revenge, searing, overwhelming hate; felt it like a physical blow.

"Well—" he decided finally—"I shall cross that bridge when I get to it . . . . and if there isn't a bridge, I'll swim . . . ."

And he grew uneasy. He wondered what would happen—and when—and why . . . .

So he gave the other back stare for stare, controlling a childish impulse to thumb his nose at the man. And then, all at once, a gong was struck—the music stopped—the whirling couples left the floor—and Colonel de Milenko stepped forward and announced:

"La Sylphe!"

Silence. He went on:

"We have persuaded La Sylphe to come here to-night—and to delight us with one of her inimitable performances."

There was applause in which Garth joined. He was excited, expectant. He moved his chair to get a better view, while a spotlight was switched on, suffusing the centre of the waxed space with a soft, golden glow.

A second later, musicians came; Tartars, bearded, voluminously turbaned, dressed in flowing robes.

They squatted on their haunches and commenced playing on native instruments—with the scraping and twanging of the *zaringhee*, the thrum-thrum-thrummy-thrum of the *zitar* and the *ut*, the bird-like fluting of the reed-pipe, the dull, grim staccato of the *tom-tom*—with a flood of strange, minor, haunting melodies, accompanied by occasional, throaty yells and baroque grace notes and gliding appoggiaturas pitched an infinitesimal sixteenth below the main harmonic notes to which the European ear is attuned.

Suddenly the music peaked to a shrill, high, savage note—and, the next moment, La Sylphe appeared . . . .

She was dressed like an Indian *nautch* girl. She wore a *sari*—the shawl which a Hindu woman drapes about herself with a deft art undreamed of by Fifth Avenue and the Rue Royale—of pale-rose, silver-embroidered silk shot with orange and purple and peacock-green and bordered with seed pearls and tiny, uncut diamonds. Her legs and feet were bare. Gold anklets and armlets jingled with every movement of her lithe body. Jewels and flowers mingled in her hair.

Of course, as always, she was masked.

Fittingly masked tonight—considered Garth—before this masked company . . . .

"Ho!" she cried.

The music wailed up. She began her dance with a sideways movement, her hands stretched out, keeping time with her feet, then gliding down the curve of pointed breasts and narrow hips, again beckoning, wavering, sometimes bent back until they almost touched the arms.

It was a dance of allurement, of temptation, perfectly carried out in every gesture, unashamedly carried out. Salome might have captured the heart of Herod with such another dance. And, with an incongruous pang of jealousy, Garth heard, clear above *tom-tom* and reed-pipe, the sharp, labored breathing of the onlookers.

Then, looking up, he noticed that Prince Tomashin had stepped to the edge of the waxed space and stood there, motionless, staring at La Sylphe; and, once more, Garth was conscious of the queer sensation of being just outside of a drama enacted quite near to him—of something threatening and sinister that was about to happen, was, perhaps, in the act of happening all around him.

He became sure of it as, right then, La Sylphe danced past his table, very close to him; as, momentarily, he imagined that her eyes were flashing through the slits in her mask, were seeking his eyes with a question—a message—an appeal . . . while the music wailed more wildly and while, quickly, she jerked into a whirl, arms straight out, the palm of her left hand turned up, that of her right hand turned down, her eyes half closed, a dreamy expression on her lips.

Then, as the music became yet more ecstatic, her whirling increased in speed. Her short, wide, circular skirt swept around and around like a great wheel. Her little bare, sweat-drenched heels made a hissing sound as they tapped the floor. Her scarf, skilfully tossed from side to side, up and down, then forward with a sweeping motion of her whole body, assumed fantastic, ever-changing shapes—soaring in a foamy cloud of purple-shaded rose, waving like a palm tree in the meeting of winds, standing up straight like a sword.

The jewels glistened. The bangles tinkled. There was a glimpse of white flesh. Everything was barbaric, sensuous, seductive . . . . and Garth, leaning forward, watching eagerly, was completely carried away.

Dance? This was not a dance.

This was life itself, passion, nature, an immense, cosmic pulsing and vibrating—and the music became louder and louder, the drummer beating his *tom-tom* with elbow and fist in a very thunder of hollow sound—she whirled faster and faster—and it was to Garth as if all India were gyrating before him in mad circles.

Monkey-gods, red and shameless and greedy, seemed to leap and leer above stolid, black stone bulls, knee-deep in sharply scented marigold. Age-green bronze bells seemed to clamor from unseen temples—calling the worshipers to prostrate themselves before Durga, the Goddess of the Thousand Names, the Goddess of the Thousand Lusts, the Goddess of the Thousand Tortures . . . .

It was the soul of all the East, with its cruelty and its grace, its strength and its cloying sweetness—and, straight through, its fixed, stony, eternal purpose.

Purpose, too, and again a question, an appeal, a message as, once more, she passed close to Garth's table, her scarf brushing his hands—as, once more, her eyes sought his.

Then, quickly, she receded toward the centre of the floor. She clapped her hands. And the music thinned to a sob. There was now only a shadowy, wiped-over thrum-thrummy-thrum-thrum of the *zitar*, a faint, far memory of thunder as the drummer's knuckles rubbed across the *tom-tom.*

Then silence. The dance was over. She gave a low salaam. She prepared to leave, the fringe of her shawl jerking sideways to the swing of her supple hips, her feet slurring over the ground with a slight jingling of anklets.

Came applause:

"Bravo!"

"Bravo!"

"Bravissimo!"

The applause grew. It bloated steadily. It thumped and droned. It massed into a solid phalanx of sound. There were frantic yells for an encore in half a dozen languages. They would not let her go. They increased their applause a hundred-fold—and finally she gave in.

She motioned to the musicians. Again reed-pipe and *zitar* and *zaringhee* floated out their minor, haunting harmonies. She stretched out her hands—was about to repeat the dance—when a voice called loudly:

"One moment—please!"

It was Prince Tomashin. He stepped up to her.

"Mademoiselle," he said slowly, distinctly, "suppose you take off your mask . . . .?"

She shrank back.

"No, no," she stammered.

"Let's see what you look like," he insisted. "Come—take off your mask . . . ."

"Sure—take off your mask!" a drunken man echoed. So did others:

"Take off your mask!"

"Take it off!"

"No, no, no!" she cried.

She turned to run away; and, quickly, true to mob psychology the world over, the crowd's admiration changed to ridicule and dislike. Why—who was she—this hired performer—that she had to surround herself with all this silly, damn-fool mystery—wearing a mask on the stage—a heavy veil when she went out in public . . . .? Say—let's take a look at the girl! Let's see if she's pretty, if her eyes are brown or blue, her nose straight or crooked . . . .

"Take off your mask!"

"Take it off!"

"Take it off!"

"Mademoiselle," said Tomashin, "the demand seems to be unanimous."

Suddenly, brutally, he reached up, about to snatch the mask from her face—when Garth interfered rapidly. Nor did the latter have to remember his promise to Sir Pascal: that he must help La Sylphe if she should need help, that he must watch, use his own judgment, act as he considered right.

Of course she needed him—and he knew what was right, promise or no promise.

He jumped up; he hurried across the room; he sent his fist crashing to the point of Tomashin's jaw; and the other dropped, knocked out cold . . . .

At once half a dozen men rushed up, members of the club, Wallachians. They were furious, threatening; and Garth thought that it looked like the beginning of a fight with the odds greatly against him. He thought, furthermore, that discretion was the better part of valor and that, were he sensible, he would make a dash for door and safety.

But how could he—how could any romantic young man—be sensible with La Sylphe so close to him, sobbing, burying her face in her hands . . . .?

He put himself in front of the girl, arms spread wide, as if to protect her. And, the next moment, there was—almost—stark tragedy.

For Malik had run in from the lobby, revolver in hand. He pulled the trigger. But the shot went wild—thanks to Colonel de Milenko who knocked the weapon aside.

"Don't do that, Malik!" he cried. "Don't be a fool! We don't want the police to . . . ."

Police!

The word, even more than the gun play, brought the guests of the club, who heretofore had rather enjoyed the excitement, to a realization of what they were up against: scandal; juicy newspaper headlines; journalists licking their reportorial or editorial chops; French equivalents of American tabloids besmirching names fair and names not quite so fair for the sake of circulation.

So, now, there was fear and pandemonium and a babel of agitated voices.

Women's faces growing pale, beneath powder and paint. Stoop-shouldered young men trying to keep their necks stiff. Hard-faced men trying to keep the flint in their eyes. Presently, men and women panic-stricken; rushing toward the exit, together with the servants, the waiters, the musicians; pushing, pressing, hurting each other in their mad haste to get out. Paleolithic warrior kicking South Sea cannibal queen. Madame Pompadour scratching George Washington. Pierrette tripping Napoleon. Cleopatra sending crashing elbow into Gretchen's tender adipose. Portuguese gentlemen dressed as Arab sheik engaging in a fist fight with Teutonic gentleman dressed as Uncle Sam—and winning a quick decision thanks to methods quite unknown to the late Marquess of Queensberry.

A surging, hysterical mass of motley costumes and masked faces, broken here and there by women's white, naked shoulders—shoulders reddening as frantic hands clawed and gripped and tore—and then Colonel de Milenko jumping up on a table, imploring them, in stentorian accents, not to lose their heads, shouting above the clamor:

"Please—please—there is no danger . . . ."

At once, typically, amazingly, as the panic had come, so it stopped.

Quietly the guests filed out. Already they began to jest about the affair; already imagined how, on the morrow, they would impress envious friends with the melodramatic telling of it; already regained a veneer of breeding with:

"After you, my dear baron."

"Did I step on your foot? So frightfully sorry, *principessa mia!*"

Garth, in the meantime, whispered a word to La Sylphe:

"Get into your street clothes—quick. I'll wait for you—take you home . . . ."

She thanked him in a soft, low-pitched voice and disappeared through the side door. Garth turned toward the lobby to get his overcoat. But he found his way barred by a number of men.

"Won't you be good enough to wait, Monseigneur?"

Again the "Monseigneur"—the form of address given to Continental royalty, to princes of the blood. Why—he wondered—who did they imagine he was . . . . ?

But, Monseigneur or not, polite or not, they were surrounding him; and he became aware of something sinister, something tragic, in the atmosphere, in this ring of masked faces staring at him through the narrow eye slits—and, momentarily, he felt the hair on his scalp stirring, as if drawn by a shivery wind; felt the clay-cold hand of fear gently touching his spine . . . .

CHAPTER FOUR

YES. Garth, just then, was conscious of fear. But it was the fear of a brave man; a man who, admitting the fact of its existence, resolutely refused to give way to it, and who was master of himself, calm, confident though not too confident, and ready to do the best he could.

By this time Prince Tomashin had staggered to his feet. He was talking in an undertone to Colonel de Milenko and to another Wallachian whose name the American had overheard earlier in the evening: Count Varolath, a lithe, graceful man, his shabby Pierrot costume speaking of slim purse and cheap Latin Quarter shop.

Shortly afterwards de Milenko and Varolath approached Garth.

"Monseigneur," announced the former, "you must give satisfaction to Prince Tomashin."

"Meaning . . . .?"

"A duel."

"Very well. I suppose it'll be the regulation place—the Bois de Boulogne tomorrow morning . . . .?"

"Impossible."

"Why?"

"Because—as doubtless you are aware—our club is in rather bad odor, politically. The Bois is too public a spot. And the police is bound to catch wind of the affair—to interfere . . . ."

"What else would you suggest?"

"The duel must be fought tonight — immediately—"

"But—where?"

"Here!"

Garth did not attempt to argue. Looking at the ring of masked faces, he had an idea that it was Hobson's choice: fight—or be murdered. Well—he thought—in a duel, given his skill with steel, he had at least a chance.

So he bowed.

"All right," he replied. "Suits me. Only—I have to have a second . . . ."

"Monseigneur," said Count Varolath, "let it be my privilege."

"Much obliged."

Varolath conferred with de Milenko who was acting as Tomashin's second. Then he returned to Garth, drew him aside, and told him that it would be heavy sabres, the duel to continue until one of the two combatants was killed or completely disabled.

"I tried to make it rapiers," he added. "But the colonel insisted on sabres. You see—the insulted party has the choice of weapons . . . ."

"Of course."

"I—I'm awfully sorry . . . ."

"Why—may I ask?"

"Because—oh—" in a low voice—"not *all* of us desire your death, Monseigneur."

"How perfectly charming of you, my dear Count! Even so, I fail to grasp . . . ."

"But—surely—you recall Prince Tomashin's reputation . . . ."

Garth thought rapidly. Evidently Tomashin's reputation on the field of honor was dangerous. He was, doubtless, a bravo, a killer. On the other hand, nobody here knew his, Garth Brent's, real name and identity. By the same token, nobody here could guess at his proficiency with weapons. This very ignorance —Garth considered amusedly—evened the odds in a way.

But he was uneasy about what might happen to La Sylphe; and he decided to appeal to Varolath. Somehow, instinctively, he liked the man.

"Look here," he began. "Now, about Mademoiselle . . . ."

"Don't worry," interrupted the other. "No harm shall come to her. I give you my word that I myself shall see her safely home—in case . . . ."

"In case I kick the bucket? That's what you're trying to say? Well—don't be so damned delicate!"

Varolath shrugged his shoulders.

"Your idea of humor, Monseigneur . . . ."

"You don't approve of it?"

"It is as it has always been—reckless, heedless. You have not changed."

The American smiled.

He was glad to know that he and Monseigneur—whoever the latter happened to be—had a trick of the ridiculous in common. It helped matters; helped the involuntary deception in which he was engaged; though not much. After all, a sense of humor and a black velvet half-mask made a rather flimsy veil with which to cloak his identity. Decidedly—he considered—he was skating on mighty thin ice.

Still—couldn't be helped . . . . and he lit a cigarette, while Varolath sighed as he looked up, at the centre of the room, where several men were busy with preparations for the duel, sanding the waxed floor, marking the proper distances with chalk, bringing and opening a velvet-and-ebony box that contained the heavy sabres.

"There would be no need for all this," Varolath went on in a tense whisper, "if I could persuade you to . . . ."

He switched into purring Wallachian; and Garth shook his head. He did not understand a word. But he could not tell the other. So, presuming on his strictly temporary rank of Monseigneur, he said sharply:

"Kindly speak French. I prefer it. You were saying something about persuading me—to do what?"

"Oh—you know."

Garth did *not* know. But he made up his mind to play the role as he imagined the man whom he was impersonating would have played it.

He felt a sudden, keen elation, as if he had been caught up and made a vital part of a shimmering, fantastic, incredible maze of events. He was in this drama—this melodrama—whatever it was, wherever it should lead. He must not fail to take his cue or speak his lines.

So, with a great deal of dignity, he said:

"I have decided. There is no use arguing."

Again the other sighed.

"Monseigneur," he rejoined, "I honor you for remaining loyal to what you hold right—although, personally, I cannot agree with you."

Garth bowed stiffly.

He was thrilled at the experience, the picaresque mystery lurking somewhere around the corner. It had something to do with Wallachia, with the succession to the throne. He was quite sure of it; sure, furthermore, that Sir Pascal was using him as a cat's-paw.

But what, precisely, was in the wind? Had he been gullible in listening to the financier and falling in with his plans?

Well—he asked himself—why not be gullible? It was the privilege of youth. Furthermore, it was, perhaps, an atavistic throwback to his Dutch ancestors who had sailed their crazy little sloops across the stormy Atlantic to find a passage to the red gold of

Cathay and the ivory and spices of the Indies. Those old Dutch shipmasters, too, had been gullible. They had been romantics. Nor had they discovered the sea way to Cathay and the Indies. But they had reached an unknown continent; and, at the end of their road, they had founded New Amsterdam, worth more today than gold and ivory and spices—as he, their latter-day descendant, at the end of *his* road, had found La Sylphe . . . .

Ah—he remembered what he had told Charles de Montfort: that he would do deeds for her sake—fabulous and storied deeds. And here, tonight, was the beginning of these deeds . . . .

"Monseigneur," Count Varolath's voice broke into his reverie, "the others are waiting . . . ."

"Very well."

He accompanied Varolath to the centre of the dance floor where Tomashin and de Milenko were standing, with Malik in close attendance. There was also a small, superbly bearded man who had come from the outside a few moments earlier; a man who wore no mask; doubtless—thought Garth—a Frenchman and a physician by every sign of gold-rimmed spectacles, neat bag, and general, pessimistic air; also doubtless known to the members of the club. For he exchanged greetings and smiles here and there; waved a friendly hand at Varolath, calling him by name.

But the latter paid no attention to him. He was

looking about the room, and he gave a little shudder of disgust, of nausea almost.

Flickering candles he saw. Withered flowers. An overturned chair or two. Crumpled gloves and handkerchiefs. A length of embroidery torn from a woman's frock. Broken bottles and glasses. A shivered mother-o'-pearl fan. Sticky remnants of food. Stale, cloying, sickening odors of perfume and alcohol.

"Sordid and mean and drab," was his morose comment. "Like a kiss that you buy with gold."

The American laughed.

"Spare me your second-hand Tolstoy!" he exclaimed.

But he, too, was affected by the atmosphere. He, too, was prey to melancholy imaginings.

All this—he told himself—was an apotheosis of post-war Europe—of kings and emperors and great satraps passing deathward in the dark, of shattered pomp, of split and shaken thrones. Dying Europe it was—dying without dignity or decency—tottering to a tawdry grave—decked out with paper flowers, with shoddy silks, and cheap, off-color diamonds—drunk with synthetic champagne—laughing with a harlot's shrill, obscene laughter . . . . and he thought of America, his own land, the cleaner, greener land; was, suddenly, strangely, homesick.

The next moment, with an effort, he pulled himself together as Varolath chose one of the two heavy sabres and handed it to him.

Came the sharp question:

"Gentlemen, are you ready?"

"Yes."

"Yes."

Blades crossed in the grand salute, engaging in quarte, foible to foible.

Then the challenge:

"Gentlemen, on guard!"

And so they were at it, two hard men at sword play. Right feet advanced. Arm muscles flexed. Wrists twisted. Weapons leaped forward—with quarte! tierce! quarte! flanconade! coupe! traverse!—sparkling from point to pommel like diamond pins.

On guard!

Again quarte! tierce! parry of quarte! counterparry! riposte! moulinet!

The hilts clanked savagely. The ringing of steel upon forged steel quickened to a rattle.

On guard!

Thrust!

Counterthrust!

At first Prince Tomashin was the attacker. He charged in with reckless skill and strength, with a rather cynical confidence in his own prowess; and it was clear to Garth that the man was a wicked fighter, a killer.

Yet, after a minute or two, Tomashin seemed surprised. He seemed a little less sure of himself—as well he might be.

For, having mistaken the young American's identity, the latter's amazing proficiency with the sabre came to him as a shock. Thus, presently, he changed his tactics. He fought more warily, more on the defensive—while, rapidly turning the tables, it was Garth who attacked—and while, on all sides, the club members were looking on, in their motley costumes, their faces covered by black velvet half-masks, their breathing, between the clank and crackle of steel, coming sharp and harsh.

A fantastic, incredible, melodramatic scene it was—here, in this ballroom—the milieu, a short while back, of gayety and laughter and clinking glasses. Now the milieu for tragedy—with Garth and Tomashin at each other, like two dolls in some cruel old Italian marionette show: unreal, unhuman, bitter. Like two grotesque silhouettes bobbing up and down—doing a *danse macabre*, a dance of death—lunging and thrusting and feinting—feet sliding, slithering, tapping the ground with dry, hollow sounds.

On guard!

Anxiously the masked men watched the duel.

There was an undercurrent of agitated whispers as it appeared that Garth was holding his own—was more than holding his own.

"Oh—look—" the sibilant exclamation—"the Prince is giving way . . . ."

"A trick!"

"You think so . . . .?"

"I'm sure of it. I've seen him do it before. Ah—" as Tomashin returned viciously to the attack—"look—did I not tell you . . . .?"

"Yes—yes . . . ."

"Here's where Monseigneur prays to the Virgin!"

But it was not so.

For Garth parried in the Sicilian manner, with arm thrust out straight, switching rapidly to vertical moulinet. Then he went to the assault in his turn, his blade whirling a swishing, triumphant saraband.

On guard! On guard!

Steadily Tomashin receded. Steadily, extending and lunging, the American advanced, until it was evident that the killer had met his master.

Once more Garth feinted. He lunged with staccato riposte, one-two, one-two.

Almost he had the other at his mercy.

And then suddenly—and, even in the fraction of that grim, bitter moment, the American felt sure that it was by a prearranged signal—Malik leaped upon Count Varolath and disarmed him; at the same time Colonel de Milenko rushed at Garth and tore the sabre from his grasp; while Tomashin moved forward swiftly, blade raised high.

"Monseigneur," he cried exultantly, "commend your soul to God!"

So death was in the air—murder bloody and unashamed—murder that did not materialize.

For, a few minutes earlier, unbeknown to the excited crowd, La Sylphe had come through the side door, dressed for the street, her face heavily veiled. She had watched the duel. At first she had been afraid. Then her fear had disappeared in the thrill of the combat. Silently, in her heart, she had cheered Garth on to victory.

Now she beheld stark treason. She beheld Garth helpless. She had no time to think; had only time to act.

There, at her feet, was a blue glint of steel. The revolver which de Milenko had knocked from Malik's hand when the latter had tried to shoot Garth.

She saw it; and—her eyes telegraphing to her brain, her brain to her hands—she picked it up. She pulled the trigger; and—was it blind luck or true aim?—the bullet struck Tomashin's sabre with a high, steely ring and jerked it out of his grip.

It flew from his hand like a shooting star; describing a glittering, fantastic curve above the heads of the onlookers; diving, point foremost, into a corner of the room where the shadows trooped thick and purple—while, a second later, the American pushed Colonel de Milenko out of the way, rushed over to La Sylphe, and ranged himself by her side . . . .

There is, in every dramatic situation, always one detail—and, occasionally, a trivial, unimportant one—which, for hidden, psychological reasons, seems lasting, more telling and poignant than the rest.

To Garth, as he took the smoking pistol from the girl's hand and waved it in slow semi-circles, covering the throng, this detail was, curiously, the attitude of the small, bearded physician.

The man appeared to be neither shocked nor frightened nor even surprised. He stood there, stout legs wide apart, swaying a little in his hips, smoking a rankly smelling French cigarette, and observing the scene with a sort of impersonal, academic amusement, as if foul play and knavery and assassination were ordinary, every-day occurrences in a physician's ordinary, every-day practice—and as if fantastic intrigues of arrant treachery, fantastic counter-intrigues of young women popping out of the nowhere and brandishing blazing revolvers, were subjects too commonplace to cause as much as a passing ripple of amazement.

"Oh la la . . . ." he murmured softly, gently, and ashed his cigarette with meticulous care.

The man's behavior made Garth feel rather foolish, rather melodramatic. Somehow, it made the gleaming revolver appear futile and ludicrous.

So, quite logically, he grew furious and, quite illogically, was on the point of expressing to the doctor, to this quite indifferent outsider, his hate and disgust, when he heard the girl sighing.

He inclined his head toward her.

"Afraid?" he asked in a low voice.

"Of course I'm afraid."

"Of course you're nothing of the sort."

"I know whether I am or not."

"Don't be silly! Why—you're a brave little girl—you saved my life . . . ."

"I suppose," Prince Tomashin cut in loudly, arrogantly, "that presently you will have finished whispering to each other . . . .?"

Then the American turned on him. He turned on all the members of the club, with icy rage, with volcanic contempt, with withering invective, with a ferocious and acrid eloquence, each carefully chosen word like the sting of a whip, each carefully rounded sentence a scarlet welt, reserving the worst insults for Prince Tomashin—who stood there, silent, thinly smiling; who, when finally Garth stopped, out of breath, calmly admitted the charge of treachery and added:

"Why should *you* complain about treachery, Monseigneur? You—who are an expert at . . . ."

"You are wrong," cut in Count Varolath. "There is a great deal of difference between treachery and honest conviction . . . ."

"Difference in cause, not in effect," came the sardonic rejoinder. "In fact, honest conviction, through its very honesty, is often more dangerous than treachery—dangerous because it is so rare, therefore unexpected—dangerous to one's class, one's principles, to everything one believes decent and proper . . . ."

The man spoke with a certain hard, ringing sincerity. Garth Brent felt this. He was interested as well as mystified.

What did it all mean—he wondered—and who was he supposed to be? What, besides faces, were those masks hiding? What brooding, tragic intrigues? What stern conflict of stern ideals . . . .?

He remembered what Sir Pascal had told him:

"A conflict of right—and right . . . ."

Then Tomashin, who had stepped up to him and away from the crowd, interrupted his thoughts.

"Surely," he demanded, "you will agree with me that it is one's duty to eliminate the enemies of the cause which one holds sacred . . . .?"

"By fair means or foul?" was Garth's ironic query.

"You will grant that I used the fair means first. For I crossed swords with you."

"Being convinced that I had never a chance?"

"Precisely. I was willing to kill you—ah—fairly, if such a thing exists. De Milenko, being a sentimentalist, insisted that I should make the attempt. But I am a careful man. I made certain preparations . . . ."

"With the help of the same—sentimentalists?"

"Yes. And so, when to my utter amazement you turned out to be the better swordsman—well—what else was I to do?"

Momentarily Garth was amused at Tomashin's chilly effrontery, his callous cynicism. Queerly, in spite of what had passed, he did not dislike him. The man was so superbly himself, so superbly master of himself. He gave a little laugh while the other went on:

"Let's call a halt to this silly situation. After all, there's nothing to keep you and Mademoiselle here any longer. I tried to kill you. I did not succeed. That's all there is to it."

"Oh—is it?"

"Isn't it?"

"You see—I might . . . ."

"Turn the tables and shoot me in cold blood? You're not the sort."

"I didn't mean that."

"What else?"

"I might call the police . . . ."

"And tell them—what, Monseigneur? Let's suppose the police should take your word and Mademoiselle's against mine—against the testimony of all the members of this club? Even so—tell me—are you willing to risk the publicity, the exposure? Is Mademoiselle . . . .?"

"No, no!" exclaimed La Sylphe. "Please—" to Garth—"let's go!"

"As you wish."

Tomashin preceded them toward the door.

"The game is not yet over," he said. "Doubtless—soon—we'll play another round."

"Again with marked cards?" countered the American.

"Why not? Marked cards make winning so much

more easy. I—please believe me—I do not like to cheat, in a game of cards or a game of life. But—" and Tomashin spoke with deep earnestness—"the stake —it is important—it is vital—don't you think . . . .?"

Here was a question which Garth, not knowing intent or meaning, decided to treat as rhetorical. So he said nothing as he accompanied the others into the hall.

All the servants had left, except Malik. The street door was half-open. Drawn up against the kerb was a low-slung motorcar, evidently a speedy, powerful machine, painted a bright robin's-egg blue.

"It's mine," explained Thomashin. "I'll be glad to drive you home . . . ."

"No—thanks."

"Afraid I might wreck the machine on purpose—and break your neck? Needn't worry, Monseigneur. I respect my own life—if I don't respect yours. Well—" as again the American refused the offer—"suit yourself."

He turned to Malik.

"Get a taxi," he ordered.

Malik hurried off; and the three—Tomashin, Garth, and La Sylphe—were alone in the lobby, near the threshold. They were silent, looking out into the street.

It was early morning. The horizon was flushing with delicate pastel shades, coral-pink and rose-pink and mauve and elfin-green. Paris was beginning to awaken, to make ready for another day's toil and sorrows and joys. Signs of life appeared here and there: workmen on their way to factories; bakers homeward bound from their hot, odorous cellars; milk wagons clattering noisily over the cobblestones; and, of course, *camelots*, newspaper boys, a ragged crew running about with their stacks of damp, early editions, yelling:

"*La Patrie!*"

"*Le Petit Parisien!*"

"*Le Matin!*"

"*Le Figaro!*"

Some of the boys stopped when they saw the three exotic figures on the threshold of the Club of the Failures. They pointed grimy fingers. They made slangy, pungent remarks. They laughed rudely, boisterously. And Garth, for one, did not blame them.

Rather unreal—he thought—this whole thing. Rather unlikely and implausible. He standing here, masked and costumed, with Tomashin, also masked and costumed, and the girl thickly veiled. And this undercurrent of tense, sultry tragedy of which he knew neither the beginning nor the end; and the adventures of the past few hours . . . . queer they had seemed in the night; seemed more queer now, in the honest light of young day.

Like going to a motion picture theater—he said to himself—and arriving in the middle of some fantastic Hollywood interpretation of life. Not knowing what the screen drama was all about. Ignorant of plot and characters. Yet deeply interested. Waiting eagerly for the beginning of the picture to come round again . . . .

"Don't forget your overcoat," Tomashin reminded Garth. "The taxi'll be here any moment."

"All right."

The American went over to the rack. He found his raglan, threw it about his shoulders, and rejoined the others in time to hear Tomashin say to La Sylphe:

"I repeat—I am sorry I made that scene—sorry I tried to snatch the mask from your face . . . ."

"How can you lie so?"

"I'm not lying. I did it on the spur of the moment."

"Why? Why?"

"Because of Monseigneur. I had decided that he must not leave the club alive. And here was a sure way of forcing a quarrel on him . . . ."

"It was cowardly!"

"But necessary."

"Necessary!" she echoed. "How I know that word. Oh—you have not changed, Maxime!"

"I have not changed—in anything. Not even in my devotion to you."

She grew angry.

"Don't talk to me," she exclaimed.

"Listen . . . ."

"No, no. I came here as a professional dancer—

because your club paid me well. But had I known . . . ."

"Had you known that I would be here you would not have come. That's precisely why my name did not appear on the invitation. But," he continued, with a great, driving appeal, "I wanted to see you again. Not on the stage. These last few weeks—and I knew from the first who you were—I watched you often on the stage, I wrote to you . . . ."

"I never replied."

"I know. And so I thought—if I could see you face to face—have a chance to talk to you . . . ."

"You did talk to me when you took me to the dressingroom. And I told you . . . ."

"That you have forgotten—everything . . . ."

"Yes."

"You—you mean it?"

"I do, Maxime."

"There are not even memories?"

"Not even memories. Only . . . ."

"What?"

"Dislike."

"You are hard."

"I am just, Maxime."

They were silent. They stared at each other.

They seemed hardly aware of Garth's presence—Garth who was more mystified than ever; who was conscious of a sharp pang of jealousy as he asked himself what was in back of all this by-play; asked himself what, in the past, there had been between La Sylphe and Tomashin . . . .

The latter turned to him now. He spoke with obvious irony:

"Your spies are clever. But—you didn't find him after all—did you?"

Find whom—? wondered Garth; and, hoping he might draw out the other, he answered:

"Did I *try* to find him?"

"No."

"Well—then . . . .?"

"I did not give you the chance. I had you watched from the first. You disguised your voice successfully. And the mask helped—of course. But the decoration on your chest—it gave you away. Tell me, Monseigneur—was it an oversight—or your old vanity . . . .?"

Garth did not reply. He shrugged his shoulders, grateful to the French who had taught him that vague, quite meaningless, and quite satisfactory gesture.

CHAPTER FIVE

JUST then a taxicab rounded the corner. It came to a stop a foot or two in back of Tomashin's car.

Malik jumped out.

The man was terribly excited. His hand clutched a crumpled newspaper. His voice peaked to a shrill, ludicrous squeak:

"Prince Tomashin—Prince Tomashin . . . ."

"What's the matter?" asked the latter.

"The Figaro—" waving the morning paper—"I found it in the taxi—I read . . . ."

His throat contracted, refused to utter the words; and Tomashin grew impatient:

"Go on—for God's sake!"

"You—oh—" stammered Malik—"you remember the plane that crashed down—yesterday . . . .?"

"Near Lyons?"

"Yes . . . ."

"Well . . . .?"

"They identified the passenger—the wounded passenger . . . . he is—Monseigneur . . . ."

"Eh . . . .?"

"Yes, yes . . . . Monseigneur—he's in the hospital—at Lyons . . . ."

"But—" Tomashin pointed at Garth—"this—this other . . . ."

"Is a liar!" shouted Malik. He faced Garth; shook his fist at him. "Liar! Impostor!"

"I'm nothing of the sort," laughed the American.

"Liar—liar—liar!"

"Aren't you the nasty, rude little man! And so frightfully unjust. Why—you didn't ask me my name . . . . nobody did . . . ."

"I'm asking you now!" cried Tomashin. "Who—who are you . . . ."

"Witness refuses to answer."

"Who are you? I want to know. Who are you?"

"Try and find out!"

And, rapidly, Garth whispered to La Sylphe. He rushed her away from the threshold and across the pavement; not to the taxicab, but to Tomashin's roadster, since it was in front of the other car, was, therefore, giving him the advantage in getting away.

She leaped in. He followed; started the engine; was off.

Instinctively he glanced over his shoulder. He saw several club members, attracted by the commotion, hurry into the lobby. He saw Tomashin and Malik enter the taxicab. He heard the former offer the chauffeur a hundred francs, two hundred francs, three hundred, if he could catch up with the roadster.

The Frenchman was more than willing.

"Citizen," he declared, "for three hundred francs I would kiss Queen Mary of England."

He stepped on the gas.

"*En avant, cocotte!*" he yelled enthusiastically.

He drove at that reckless speed for which Paris taxicab men are famous as well as infamous, admired as well as feared; and Garth, although the roadster was fast and he an expert behind the wheel, had his work cut out trying to increase the distance. And he knew that he must increase it. For Tomashin would have to be kept from finding out where he lived; would have to be kept, by the same token, from discovering his identity. Not because he, personally, was afraid of the man. But he knew instinctively, for reasons which, just then, he had not the time to analyze, that his incognito, where Tomashin was concerned, would be vital to La Sylphe.

He turned to the right, into a spider's web of narrow, crooked, cobblestoned streets and alleys that entangled itself about the ancient Church of Saint Sulpice and where he could play hide-and-seek with the pursuers.

Streets answering to names flavored with a certain quaint, provincial charm: rue Palatine, rue Garancière, rue Férou, rue Servandoni. Old, sad, silent streets. So silent that the mewing of some dusty ashbin cat, the twittering of a canary hanging in its cage from a kitchen window, or the tinkly bell of a knife-sharpener's pushcart struck the ear with the force of a sudden blow; so silent that the roar of the two racing cars sounded like thunder.

Streets quiet with the quiet of death.

Yet once these same streets had seen the history of France in the making, the unmaking, the remaking. For there, during the Terror, the proscribed aristocrats had gone in search of refuge and asylum. There the ragged, wool-capped hangmen of Robespierre had ferreted them out and dragged them forth to lamp-post and guillotine and the potter's field. There, in the shadow of the Church of Saint Sulpice, a pitiful few had hidden their powder-bags, their brocaded coats, their lace jabots, their jeweled snuff-boxes, their simpering love-letters, and their worn-out, feudal ideals.

Ideals—thought Garth—like those of the Wallachian noblemen back there in the Club of the Failures; the royalists; the adherents of the old régime . . . . and again he wondered—speculated about the Why and Wherefore, about La Sylphe's connection with the whole mystery . . . .

He glanced at her. She glanced back; smiled.

"Where do you live?" he asked.

"At the Excelsior."

A faint, soft laugh was in her voice; and he liked her the more because of it. Evidently she had courage —courage already proved by the incident with the pistol—and, as evidently, she was enjoying the keen elation of the chase quite as much as he.

For—no doubt—he was enjoying it.

"A fair field and no favors!" the slogan of the green turf popped into his mind.

Yes. A fair field. Here it was as, suddenly, at full speed, pursued by the taxicab, he twisted out of the rabbit's-warren of alleys and shot down a long, smooth stretch of tree-lined boulevard, caring never a tittle for the white-gloved hands of gendarmes excitedly and ineffectually raised.

On, then!

Jerking past top-heavy motorbus and early delivery cart. Shaving a milk wagon piled high with rattling cans. Scattering a crowd of blue-bloused workmen. Swerving drunkenly to save a small boy who was sitting on the kerb and munching a penny roll with the stolid, solemn satisfaction of childhood. Presently leaving the boulevard and turning south through a crowded faubourg. Causing the air to ring with cries of terror as he boomed past groups of midinettes. Forcing a suburban egg-merchant's mare to rear and plunge and the driver to swear in memorable, vitriolic French. Tooting his reckless way amidst the motley throngs that give zest and meaning to these old streets: water-carriers, knife-grinders, glaziers, peddlers of rabbit-skins, menders of broken crockery—indeed so broken that none but a French housewife would dream of having them glued and wired.

Still on!

Some of the people were angry at the speeding automobile. They shook their fists and cursed and threatened. Others were amused; and, typically, tolerantly French, willing to live and let live, catching a glimpse of the American's velvet face mask and his fur cap with the tall aigrette, they decided that "*Monsieur a fait la noce*," that, in other words, he had been out on a bat.

Wittily, slangily, they commented on it, reminding Garth that his costume was making him conspicuous, easy to trace if Tomashin should stop his car and ask questions. So he removed mask and cap; crammed both down at the bottom of the roadster; felt safer, since his raglan completely covered the cherry-red tunic.

Again he glanced at La Sylphe.

So sweet—the curve to her chin.

And he wondered what she was thinking about; said to her, his voice rising above the roar of the engine:

"A penny for your thoughts!"

"Are you quite sure my thoughts aren't worth more than a penny?"

"Maybe they are."

"And maybe they aren't. For—you see—I am thinking of you."

"And what, in particular, are you thinking—of me?"

"I'm thinking—seeing you without the mask—that you are English."

"Don't be so insulting!"

"Oh . . . ."

"I'm an American."

"You're the first American I've ever met."

"Well—I'm a splendid specimen of a splendid race."

She laughed. He told her his name; went on:

"Turn about is fair play. What is *your* name?"

"La Sylphe."

"Please . . . ."

"Don't you like it?"

"Tremendously. It is charming—adorable. But I mean—your real name . . . ."

She shook her head. Nor did he insist. He smiled. He thought that he had a way of finding out—through Charles de Montfort, who was employed in the Bureau of Registry; that amazingly efficient French government department which, from a political more than from a strictly criminal point of view, is the very heart of the republic.

For there lives hardly a prominent man or woman in France, foreign or native, who has not his or her card or a whole nest of cards—*bordereaux* they are called officially—in the underground, steel filing-cabinets of the Bureau of Registry in the rue de Berri . . . . each card containing a man or woman's life history; a record, often, of old, far-off, unhappy, forgotten things; forgotten, perhaps, by the very people to whom they happened—though never forgotten by the Bureau . . . .

Oh yes. He would ask Charles . . . .

"Mademoiselle La Sylphe," he said suddenly.

"Yes . . . .?"

"Weren't you startled when you discovered that I am not Monseigneur."

"No."

"No . . . .?"

"I knew, before I went to the club, that the real Monseigneur had been injured . . . ."

"Well—I'll be . . . ."

"Damned?" she suggested.

"Exactly. By the way, Monseigneur means Royal Highness, doesn't it? Royal Highness of what particular lot of European real estate?"

She hesitated; and he added:

"You might as well tell me. I can find out so simply—by taking a look at the morning paper—the airplane accident, you know . . . ."

She replied:

"Monseigneur is Karolus."

"The former Crown Prince of Wallachia?"

"Yes."

"I had a hunch like that straight along. I thought it was either Karolus—or that other royal bird—what's his name?—Prince Danielo . . . ."

He was silent as he glanced back and saw the taxicab increase its speed. He did likewise. He turned away from the faubourg; cutting through the ring of outer boulevards which tops the old fortifications; descending into the lean valley where Paris ends and where suburbia begins with chicken-coops and home-made garages and scraggly, weedy, miserable vegetable gardens.

After a while he asked:

"Tell me something else."

"If I can."

"When you danced past my table—you had no idea who I was?"

"Not the slightest."

"Then why did you look at me the way you did?"

"What way?"

"Sort of—oh—as if you needed my help . . . ."

"I didn't."

"You bet you did!"

"All right—I admit it."

"Because of Tomashin?"

"Yes. He talked to me . . . ."

"When he took you to the dressingroom. I know. And I suppose—" sharply, jealously—"he made love to you?"

Her words were just as sharp as his:

"Is it any of your business?"

"I beg your pardon, Mademoiselle."

She looked at him from beneath lowered eyelids. He seemed sulky. And, quickly, she reconsidered, reversing her emotions with strictly feminine agility. Why—she thought—she had been angry at him because of his jealousy. She was angry no longer. On the contrary, she was delighted. She gave a little giggle; continued:

"Incidentally—you're mistaken. He did not make love to me. At least not precisely. But something he said—it frightened me—I needed a friend—and I saw . . . ."

"My honest face?" he jested, good-humored again. "So honest that it shone through my mask?"

"No. I saw the decoration on your tunic."

Garth drew in his breath. The decoration—he reflected—on which Tomashin had commented and which had so startled Malik . . . .

"Important decoration?" he inquired.

"Very important. Indeed almost unique. Where did you get it?"

"At a pawnbroker's," replied the American, remembering his promise to Sir Pascal.

"I don't believe you."

"Calling me a liar—in other words?"

"Yes."

"What a rude little girl you are!"

He laughed. So did she. She said:

"Anyway—I needed help, needed a friend—and I found you—and I am grateful . . . ."

"Not half as grateful as I. You saved my life. And so—I'd like to make the score a little more even."

"How?"

"I would like to help you some more. You're in trouble, aren't you?"

"I am."

"Tell me all about it."

"I can't."

"Please!"

"I haven't the right to involve you in my affairs, Mr. Brent."

"My friends call me Garth. And, as to your affairs, seems to me I'm involved already . . . ."

He was silent as, again glancing over his shoulder, he saw the taxicab speeding up; heard the jeering, sardonic tooting of its horn, as if trying to warn him:

"I'll catch up with you soon!"

Garth pumped gas into the engine. He streaked ahead with a sensation as if he were endeavoring to lift the roadster along the pavement by sheer strength of muscle and tendon.

Then, suddenly, the chase came to an end.

For, taking a corner at a terrific pace, at nearly right angles, on two wheels, the American saw a great, gaunt house jutting abruptly into the focus. Too, around this same corner, directly across from the building, he saw the road, too narrow to allow a free curve, dipping to a deep cleft which was crowned by an embankment.

Somehow he succeeded in negotiating the curve and avoiding house as well as embankment.

But the taxicab did not.

It missed the house. But it flew up the steep bank on the other side of the road as if on iron wings—and the American heard a choked cry of fear, of horror. At once he put down the brake. He turned round—looked—just as the taxicab, within an inch of the top of the embankment, slithered to a stop—seemed to hang, to swing in mid-air—for an eternity . . . .

Then, simultaneously with three figures catapulting through the air, the taxicab fell. It twisted sideways, describing a fantastic somersault. It smashed down on the pavement. It bounced like a rubber ball. It smashed again, upside down—and there was the crunching of tortured steel, of maimed, crushed tubes and wheels . . . .

At this moment Garth did not consider that Tomashin and Malik were his enemies from whom he was trying to escape. He only considered that they were human beings, that they needed help.

And he jumped out of the roadster. He ran back along the road, toward the scene of the catastrophe.

There already a crowd had gathered. As always, as if by magic, a doctor was amongst.

Excitement. Exclamations:

"Ah—the unfortunates!"

"Dear Virgin!"

"Fools! That comes from this reckless driving!"

"People have no sense!"

A woman broke into hysterical sobs.

A white-haired priest crossed himself and began intoning the:

"O Sanctissima . . . ."

The physician was bending over the three prone figures. He made a swift examination with skilled, nervous hands. Then—rather proudly, rather as if he were claiming credit for it—he pronounced judgment:

"Bruised. Cut. Shaken up. But—they'll be as right as rain in no time."

"A miracle—*hein?*"

It was the old priest speaking; and, immediately, the doctor, being an orthodox atheist by profession, forgot the injured men and considered it his scientific duty to contradict the other.

"A miracle?" he sneered. "Pah! Pap for puling infants—and for sexless, toothless old hags. Personally I believe in . . . ."

"In nothing," interrupted the priest. "Not even in yourself—eh? Will you permit a foolish servant of Holy Church to point out to you that it is such a vain, silly gesture to shake your fists at the eternal stars—and to expect them to topple down at your command?"

"Oh—listen to me . . . ."

"Why should I? I know what you are going to say. You are going to say that you have seen God die—that you have witnessed His demise. And my reply is that a blind man is not a very reliable eye witness . . . ."

Thus the priest scored; and the physician grew angry. He waved his hands; started to argue; was silenced by a large, red-faced butcher who cried:

"We need an ambulance . . . ."

"Yes . . . ."

"There's a hospital in the rue Chauveau—it's quite near . . . ."

"I'll telephone . . . ."

So the ambulance was called, while Garth returned to his car and told La Sylphe what had happened. They drove on at a more leisurely pace and reached the Hotel Excelsior twenty minutes later.

It was the usual sort of ultra-modern caravanserai which the New World's demandful—and well-paying—tourists have forced on the Old World.

Marble and waiters from Italy. Chefs and bronzes from Alsace. Pastry crooks from Vienna. Porters from Normandy and the Midi. Barkeepers from Chicago. Kitchen wenches from the Levant and the Isles of Greece. Vases from Japan and Saxony. Rugs from Persia and New Jersey. Furniture from England and Norway. Dutch silver. Belgian glass. Irish linen. And American the bathtubs and plumbing and cocktail recipes and ice water at all hours.

American, furthermore, though with a spice of British Colonial, the money that clinked across the counter.

But of the French, French, the hand that received this same money.

French the one hundred million francs investment. French every single centime of the profits. French the charges—and over-charges. French the mixture of politeness and arrogance, the blending of fantastic luxury and fantastic greed.

Typically French . . . .

And typical, too, the early morning scene in the lobby—the few stray, lonely human beings that seemed so tiny and unimportant and rather pathetic in the immense, cathedral-like rotunda.

For instance, a burly but diplomatic house detective endeavoring to pacify an intoxicated visitor from the wilds of Western Australia who pulled off the hoary old saw that—hic!—he had been kicked outa—hic!—a bloody lot o' a bloody sight sweller places than this 'ere—hic!—bloody dump . . . .

A gray-haired Breton scrubwoman on her knees, crooning to herself in her queer Keltic way that—*bon Dieu!*—once, back home in Britanny, she had heard a nightingale warbling so sweet; and—ah!—the lovely tune it had been and the pretty, pretty wee bird . . . .

A nostalgic commercial traveler from Illinois, waiting for the taxicab to take him to the boat train, lolling in an armchair, and reading in a fortnight-old home tabloid how, in his death cell, the doomed Red Kid had eaten a last, hearty breakfast consisting of beefsteak and onions and German-fried potatoes, and how Professor Copernicus W. Saltenstall, the eminent psychologist, had finally been run to earth in his suburban love nest, with a volume of W. Somerset Maugham's "Of Human Bondage," a quart of fairly decent Bourbon whiskey, an illustrated brochure on sex hygiene, and a co-ed with yellow, bobbed hair and romantic leanings . . . .

Other people.

Not many.

One man who stood near the entrance. A fairly tall, slim man, in a loose, long, pepper-and-salt overcoat, a slouch hat pulled well over his forehead so that his features were shadowed and indistinct.

He was leaving as Garth and La Sylphe entered. He passed them on the threshold. He brushed against the American—who gave a start of surprise. For the stranger had passed something into his hand.

Rapidly Garth glanced over his shoulder. The other had already disappeared down the street.

"What is it?" asked La Sylphe.

"Oh—nothing . . . . I thought—I thought I knew that man . . . ."

Should he run after him?

No—he decided. He did not wish to alarm the girl. But he was curious. So, following her through the lobby, he took a surreptitious look at what the stranger had given him. It was a small piece of thin paper. Written on it—or, rather, awkwardly printed —was the message:

> "Keep out of this if you value your life.
> One who is not your enemy—yet."

The "yet" was underlined.

Garth stuffed the paper into his pocket.

He was disturbed, nervous, uneasy. Somehow the thought that he was being watched made him feel guilty; unreasonably guilty; as, during the war, shadowing German spies, he had always felt guilty at the realization that they, in their turn, were watching him.

But he dismissed it from his mind. Right now—he considered—he had another matter to attend to: a personal and vital matter.

For there was this girl. He liked her so much. He must tell her—oh—things . . . .

She walked straight toward the elevator shaft. She extended a hand as if to wish him "au revoir"—a hand which he refused to take.

Instead he took her arm; led her to a corner of the lobby; and said:

"I've got to talk to you."

"Some other time. You see—I'm so tired."

"Sorry. But can't be helped. I've *got* to talk to you."

"About . . . .?"

"The two most important things in the world."

"And they are . . . .?"

"Yourself—and myself."

She smiled. They sat down. The corner of the lobby was quiet, palm-screened, intimate.

"You wouldn't let me look at you—would you?" he began.

"You *are* looking," she replied. "Indeed you are staring."

"At a veil. A thick veil. Not very satisfactory."

"Have you no imagination at all?"

"You bet I have. At times more than is good for me. But I am curious to know if the facts agree with what I imagine."

"What *do* you imagine?"

"That you are very lovely."

"Oh—you disappoint me so. I had an idea you were a romantic young man. And now—such a trite, every-day compliment!"

"In self-defence."

"How so?"

"Otherwise you'd think me *too* romantic. You see —if I really told you what I imagine . . . ." He slurred; stopped; continued: "Look here—do you want me to tell you?"

"No."

"Meaning yes. Listen—" bending towards her a little, speaking low-voiced words that were tremendously, fantastically un-American—"I imagine your face finely and delicately chiseled. Soaring forward, I imagine it, as a bird soars into the wind. Like a song that Sappho might have sung to the Greeks of Rhodes—or perhaps of Cyprus—a song made of wine and honey—red wine and golden honey . . . ."

She laughed.

"You *are* romantic."

"Shamelessly so," he admitted. "But the question is: am I right—in what I imagine?"

"If I said yes, you'd think me vain."

"And you aren't vain—are you?"

"Of course not."

"Well then—let me look at your face—let me find out for myself."

"No."

"Please!"

"No, no."

"I guess I know the reason. I wager you've a wart on your nose . . . ."

"Oh—" indignantly—"I have not!"

"A wart on your nose," he insisted—"a large, brown one. And faulty adenoids. And not at all the sort of skin a mother loves to touch—and . . . ."

"I dislike you intensely."

"Can't be helped. Still—seeing is believing."

Finally she gave in. She raised her veil—and he saw a low, broad, white forehead; a whorl of russet hair accentuating the square contours of the temples;

sloe-black eyes showing deep beneath boldly hooded lids; oval features that were soft in outline, yet indicating courage and strength and independence and a certain obstinacy.

A very beautiful face—and he stared until she blushed and put back her veil—and then he asked:

"How frank may I be?"

"As frank as you please."

"You won't laugh at me?"

"I'll try not to."

"Very well. Here goes." And, being the sort of man he was, he said to her without the least embarrassment or self-consciousness: "Mademoiselle, permit me to inform you that you are like one of those lovely symbols which, so very rarely, a great and generous God shapes out of that shoddy stuff called life."

She made a little noise in her throat; and he demanded severely:

"You aren't laughing, are you?"

"I am."

"Why?"

"Because I wonder how often, in the past, you used the same words to other girls."

"Not more than twice. Maybe three times. But, today, it's different."

"Oh . . . .?"

"Today I mean it—with all my heart and soul."

"You think you mean it—because it is Paris and May and the sky so blue."

"I mean it because it's true."

He was silent for a minute or two; continued very seriously:

"You are in trouble. And I want to help you."

"No," she replied slowly, very earnestly. "You cannot help me."

"I can, too. Sorry if I'm blowing my own horn. But—you could look farther and find worse than me."

"I'm quite sure of it. But—we're strangers."

"No longer."

"Oh yes—we are. Why should you want to help me?"

"Couldn't guess why—could you?"

"Oh—" she stammered.

"All right. I'll tell you." He paused. "Again—how frank may I be?"

"Again—as frank as you please."

"Again—you won't laugh at me?"

"Again—I'll try not to."

"Fair enough." He smiled. "The reason why I want to help you is simplicity itself. You see—I love you. I love you very madly—and very sincerely . . . ."

"You fall in love—frequently?" was her mocking query.

"Well—occasionally," he admitted. "Once, when I was a boy at prep school, I fell in love with the headmaster's maiden aunt. And, when I studied at Harvard, I loved a number of blond, giggling girls whom I met here and there. Then, growing ever in years and taste and wisdom, when I was a soldier in France, I fell in love with a brown, blowsy girl from the Provence—and her love was like a laugh and a scuffle. But now—" lowering his voice—"I know that the only girl for me must have sloe-black eyes and ruddy hair and slim, white hands like riddles and a grace and a carriage to put her aside from all other women. A little girl—you might say—masquerading as La Sylphe . . . ."

She looked at him. She thought:

"I like him. I like his eyes. They are nice eyes. Steady, kindly eyes."

Aloud she said:

"You talk like a poet."

"Because, in your presence, I feel like a poet." He laughed. "Poetry on an empty stomach! Which reminds me—will you breakfast with me?"

"No—thank you."

"What about lunch?"

Once more she refused; refused a dinner invitation as well.

He remonstrated:

"Dieting is the fashion. I know. But, even so, you must eat *some* time."

"My appetite is excellent. Only—I never eat in public because . . . ."

"I understand. Because of your incognito, the veil which you insist on wearing. And I guess it's rather difficult to eat through a veil—chiefly oysters and thick soup. Well—suppose *you* invite *me*—to dine at your apartment? Shall we say tonight . . . .?"

"Not tonight. I'm too tired."

"Some other time then. Perhaps next Saturday?"

"Perhaps."

"And should you want me in the meantime—why—let me know . . . ."

He scribbled his name and address on a sheet of hotel stationery. On an impulse he wrote underneath:

"Write, telephone, wire, when you need me.
And I'll come at once—to break a lance for you."

She smiled at him. She said:

"You are nice!"

"And you are sweet!"

And he bowed, kissed her hand, and left.

CHAPTER SIX

GARTH stopped on the outer threshold of the hotel lobby and looked warily up and down the street.

For he recalled the warning message which the stranger had passed into his hand, and he considered that this same stranger—or somebody else interested in his movements—might be watching him, ready to shadow him to his residence and discover his identity. But, thanks to his former work in the Military Intelligence Service, he had a knack, akin to second sight, of sensing, more than seeing or hearing, when he was being observed; sensing it by the subtlest imaginable reflex vibrations upon his nervous system. And, presently, he told himself that the coast was clear.

Still, he decided to make assurance doubly sure.

So, suddenly, he jumped into the roadster. He was off again at a fast pace; turned and twisted to shake off possible pursuers; and, at last, was absolutely certain that nobody was following him.

He knew that it would be too risky to drive all the way home to his apartment house. For he was well known in the neighborhood. Besides, the car, with its bright, robin's-egg blue chassis, was easily spotted.

And it was on the cards that Tomashin would institute a search for it; that detectives might trail it to the Place de Fontenoy where he lived, get into conversation with butcher and baker and candlestick-maker, and receive indiscreet answers to discreet queries.

Should he abandon the automobile on the nearest deserted street . . . .?

No. His sense of honesty would not let him. Nor would his sense of humor.

He took it to a garage and left it there.

"What name?" asked the man in charge.

"Prince Tomashin," Garth replied calmly. "I'll call or send for it."

He walked down the street, his long, loose raglan covering his costume to his ankles. He had forgotten the Wallachian fur cap which he had crammed down in a corner of the roadster. So he was without a hat, but was neither aware of it nor conspicuous, since, like many Parisians, he had taken up the bare-head fad.

Just then no taxicab was near, and he strolled along for a few blocks, enjoying the fresh air, enjoying Paris.

Paris today, as always, up and about and doing at cock's-crow; today, as always, eager for life and work—exuberant life and work—energetic, emphatic, good-humored, uniquely Latin.

Crowds were pouring through the streets, bumping against each other, swapping spiced jests and spiced abuse. Artisans were there, voluminously breeched, blue-bloused, aggressively democratic. The army was there, stalking along in clumsy, bulgy boots, dragging truculent sabres, twirling mustaches, ogling the women. A sprinkling of the navy was there, and a good deal of the nursery. Cassocked priests with gentle lips and weary, wise eyes. Midinettes in black taffeta. A bent, aged Jewish peddler with pack on back who, beneath his greasy rags, succeeded in preserving the dignity and tragedy of the Old Testament. Little schoolboys, in tight trousers and bowler hats, aping their elders who, like all good Parisians, aped the English. Housewives out to buy long, yellow loaves and short, dark-green bottles. Middle-aged businessmen, comfortable, silk-hatted. Young businessmen, in all the crushing self-importance of recently acquired beards and as recently acquired bank accounts.

An unending procession, with the sound like the sound of an army marching to war with banners and drums. Stacked carts rumbling along. Heavy motor drays clattering. Workmen, naked to the waist, erecting a new building. An engine jerking up the black arms of a gigantic crane, the whistling of the escaping steam adding a dramatic undertone to the symphony of the streets.

The kerb-stones lining with impromptu, open-air stalls; the shouts of the sellers:

"Cabbage heads!"

"Red peppers!"

"Green peppers!"

"Onions!"

"Aubergines!"

"Turnips!"

"Oranges!"

The Paris—reflected Garth—of which the average American, on his eternal, hectic round between the Ritz and the Rotonde, the Bi-Ba-Bo and Fouquet's Bar, was profoundly unaware. Not the Paris of refined, expensive, and alcoholic vice; the foreigners' Paris. But the Paris of the Parisians: vulgar and crass and loud-mouthed. And, louder than all the rest, a fish-woman with high-kilted skirts and a generous display of stout, crimson-stockinged calves, holding up her tray of glistening, squirming, living wares, and giving the traditional, full-throated cry of her trade:

"*A la barque! A la barque!*"

Garth was passing. He was in a happy mood. For, when he had told La Sylphe that, for the first time in his life, he was really in love, he had spoken the truth.

So there was a glow in his soul and a smile in his eyes as, stopping to light a cigarette, he happened to look at the fish-woman . . . . jolly, she seemed, with her apple-red cheeks, her poppy-red lips . . . .

He bowed and said:

"Madame!"

She curtsied and replied:

"Monsieur!"

"Have you the faintest notion of what I'm thinking?"

"To be sure."

"Let's hear it."

"You're thinking that you wish to buy some of my fish." She held up a wiggly, fat mackerel. "A beauty—and only seven francs."

"Confound your mackerel, Madame!"

"Perhaps a brook trout?"

"Confound your trout!"

"Oh . . . .?" a bit angrily.

"Nothing personal. But—confound all your fish! You see—I'm thinking of a palace . . . ."

"What palace?"

"The one I shall build for the girl I love. A palace made of reddish-gold autumn leaves—to match the color of her hair. Charming—don't you think?"

"Perhaps. But rather draughty."

"Soulless, materialistic woman! My love will keep her snug and warm."

"Ah—" said the woman with a laugh—"you are American—therefore crazy."

"Permit me to correct you. I am American—therefore hungry. I shall now go and breakfast. You care to join me? No? I am terribly sorry." Again he bowed. "Au revoir, Madame."

"Au revoir, Monsieur."

So, at a little nearby dairy, he breakfasted very well indeed on coffee with real cream and boiled eggs and a couple of crisp crescent rolls. Then he hailed a passing taxicab; and, twenty minutes later, arrived at his apartment house which overlooked the Place de Fontenoy, with a view beyond the Pasteur monument, of the tracery of the elm-trees which bordered the square, farther on a tawny glimpse of the Champ de Mars, and, to the north, the bombastic, bragging dome of the Hotel des Invalides.

He climbed the stairs; let himself in with his latchkey; and was greeted by sonorous, accusing, and purely African accents:

"I'se been waitin' up fo' you all night, suh!"

"Silly of you, George."

George W. Brown was Garth's colored servant. He had been his striker during the war and, after demobilization, had followed him, protesting but loyal, to Paris—Paris of which he, as a hard-shell Alabama Baptist, most thoroughly disapproved. Indeed, right now, disapproval oozed out of his every pore—as he saw Garth in his gaudy Wallachian costume; reported that somebody had sent the other clothes which his employer had worn on the previous evening; pointed at the unslept-in bed in the next room; grumbled that he himself didn't hold with spending the night in strange beds; and added:

"De Lawd's gwine to visit His displeasure an' wrath on dis-heah house—wot wid dem Scribes an' Pharisees an' painted French hussies . . . ."

"You do me an injustice," laughed the other. "I

didn't sleep in a strange bed last night. In fact, I didn't go to bed at all. And, for the future, I'm off all hussies—French or otherwise. And do you know why, George?"

"You've seen de light, Cap?"

"You bet! The light of sloe-black eyes!"

He undressed and stretched out on a couch.

"Call me in a couple of hours," he continued. "Oodles of things to do today. And you might improve your French by wrestling with Central and 'phoning to M. de Montfort. Ask him to pick me up on his way to the office. And pass me that American magazine with the green cover—it's the best sleeping draught next to veronal . . . ."

It was one of those monthlies which tells the world that East is East and West is West, while the Middle West is nowhere at all; that, regardless of who may be right, My-Country-'Tis-Of-Thee is always wrong; that true culture is found exclusively in Budapest, Munich, and Patagonia; that Longfellow never wrote a single line of real poetry; that all Methodists are hypocrites and all patriots rogues; that only Tennessee half-wits read the Bible; that ex-President Calvin Coolidge was nothing but a lucky, peanut politician; that Eugene Debs' fame will outlive George Washington's; and more of the same sort.

Small wonder that Garth, being a sane extrovert, fell promptly asleep over the magazine—to be awakened, two hours later, by his servant who reported that M. de Montfort would call around ten o'clock.

Garth shaved, bathed, dressed.

In his mind he went over the happenings of the previous night. So unreal he considered them; so fantastic.

Then, on an impulse, he telephoned to his bank. Yes—the receiving teller informed him with new-born respect—early this morning one hundred thousand dollars had been deposited to the account of Mr. Brent.

Well—thought the latter—here was something quite tangible, quite real. And real, too, was the scrawled message pressed into his hand by the strange man on the threshold of the Hotel Excelsior.

He read it again:

> "Keep out of this if you regard your life.
> One who is not your enemy—yet."

A warning. Sharp and to the point. Though not precisely unfriendly.

He wondered who might have written it; told himself that, since his connection with the mystery had begun with his entering the Club of the Failures, the sender must be a member of this club.

He had met three of them: Varolath, de Milenko, and Prince Tomashin. The latter two being out of the question, it was reasonable to assume that Count Varolath was responsible for the warning. The man had known that Garth was taking la Sylphe home; had, furthermore, known her address; and, with the American driving in a roundabout way so as to escape Tomashin and Malik, had had plenty of time to reach the Excelsior ahead of the others.

On the other hand—Garth asked himself—why this warning to a stranger who, very evidently, was ranged on the side of Varolath's political enemies? Was it because Varolath was more in sympathy with Karolus' views—whatever they were—than he let on and therefore willing to help Karolus' adherents? Or was it simply that Varolath had reacted to a sudden feeling of liking, of friendship, and did not wish to see Garth harmed?

Why not?

The American reflected how he himself, immediately, had liked the other. And he reflected, too, how sudden friendship happens more often than people believe, as much between man and man as between man and woman—though these quick, almost instantaneous waves of mutual sympathy can be no more easily explained by the humanist than the instantaneous influence of radio-activity of one atom on another can be explained by the physicist.

Perhaps—thought Garth—in both cases, in the final analysis, it was the secret hand of Fate, of God.

At all events, he decided that he would thank Varolath, and so he wrote on a telegraph blank:

"Grateful for the warning.
One who will never be your enemy."

He addressed the message to Varolath in care of the Club of the Failures. Then, again obeying his sense of honesty as well as his sense of humor, he addressed a second message, unsigned, also in care of the club, to Tomashin, informing him at what garage he had left the roadster; and instructed George to send off both wires during the morning.

Shortly afterwards Charles de Montfort entered.

"Had breakfast, Charles?"

"Yes. My usual."

"Half a cup of chicory and a bad cigarette?"

"And you, I suppose, had your customary, fantastic, transatlantic repast—clam-chowder and ice-cream . . . ."

"Don't forget the chewing gum, Charles. Never mind. Do something for me?"

"Anything," was the Frenchman's mock-heroic reply, "except high treason against my country."

"Well—that's what it may amount to."

"Pardon . . . .?"

"You see—I want to know if it's possible for me, an outsider and a foreigner, to consult some of those confidential little cards at the Bureau of Registry where you are employed, Charles . . . ."

"I suppose it can be arranged—unless the cards refer to . . . ."

"State secrets?"

"Exactly."

"Try and fix it—will you?"

"Going in for the private detective racket—to earn a living?"

"No."

"Well—then . . . .?"

"Cherchez la femme!"

"Is she pretty?"

"Adorably beautiful. You'll meet her one of these days. In fact, I want you to be my best man when I . . . ."

"I thought you were crazy about La Sylphe?"

"Oh—you know what I am . . . ."

"A Mormon . . . ."

"Let's call it a Turk. Sounds more romantic. Anyway, the girl's in rather a mess. Certain people are bothering her——"

"And so, I take it, you would like to find out if you can bother these same certain people by getting the—what do you Americans call it?—the—oh . . . ."

"By getting the low-down on them. That's about it. Can you arrange it?"

"I'll see. I'll have a talk with my chief, M. Marchand. Frightful old snob. Terribly keen about

Dukes and Duchesses. Would give his right ear for an invitation to my parents' house. That's the bait I'll hold out."

"Nice of you. Can you do it right away?"

"In a hurry?"

"Yes, Charles."

"All right. Let's go."

So the two young men drove to the Bureau of Registry where Charles interviewed M. Marchand, then rejoined his friend and reported:

"I asked the chief up to the house for tea next Sunday afternoon—won't mother be furious!—then begged him to let you snoop about here and there. I told him you're a harmless idiot—just one of those nosey, inquisitive Yankees . . . ."

"Now wasn't that charming of you!"

"Did the trick—didn't it? Here's your permit. Come and meet Poret."

And Charles de Montfort introduced Garth to the latter, the official in charge of the files, a tall, cadaverous, sardonic man, who led the way to the immense basement of the Bureau of Registry, while Charles returned to his office.

The basement, which stretched underground for blocks and covered almost two acres, was entered by intricate doors like those of a safe. Inside it was steel-walled, steel-ceilinged, and steel-floored. The whole place resembled an enormous safety-deposit vault.

It was continuously patrolled by armed guards, protected by elaborate chemical and electric devices, and the pressure of a single button would flood it with water, within three minutes, from floor to ceiling. Around the walls, from top to bottom, were great steel filing cabinets, each provided with an ingenious lock; and, bending over low, flat tables, a number of men, who seemed more like elderly, scholarly librarians than headquarters employees deep in secrets of state, were busy with small pasteboard cards—red cards and yellow and blue and white and green—writing, comparing, filing away . . . . "collecting confidential data contributed by hundreds of operatives," explained Poret.

"Keeping tabs on criminals?" asked Garth.

"No."

The American was surprised.

"No . . . .?" he echoed.

"Keeping tabs on—mostly—quite decent people. But people who are prominent or who might some day become prominent—or who are merely unusual, out of the ordinary rut. And, chiefly, keeping tabs on people who are ambitious."

"Is ambition a danger?"

"To a democracy? Decidedly. That is if the ambition is—well . . . ."

"Too personal?"

"That's it," agreed Poret. "And so we watch—listen—observe—collect . . . ."

"What?"

"Everything," replied the other, with a sort of cynical pride. "Everything—from a man's first attack of chicken-pox to his last attack of delirium tremens, from the state of his bank balance to that of his uric acid. These cards give a concise résumé of any political opinions he may have uttered, a report of his married life, his taste in wine, women, and drugs, his virtues, his hobbies and his vices, his favorite restaurants, his friends, his enemies, and—of course—his illegitimate children and his mistresses."

"And the cards relating to women . . . .?"

"No difference. Except that, naturally, for mistresses we substitute lovers if the woman be young—and gigolos if she be old . . . ."

The system is like an immense spider's web, stretching everywhere. It is complete in every detail. By comparison, Scotland Yard is a child's house of cards, and the United States Secret Service, Russia's *Ogpu*, and Berlin's *Polizei Presidium* are studies in inefficiency.

France hates it; fears it; yet is proud of it, knowing that it is the safety valve which, more than once, in the past, has saved the country from treason and revolution and catastrophe.

For let an enemy of the republic, be he communist or royalist, financial adventurer or military adventurer, attempt to overthrow the government—and, frequently, there will be no need of force to pull his teeth. Just a name given to one of these elderly, scholarly clerks in the basement of the Bureau of Registry; a card—red, white, green, or yellow—taken from one of the many steel filing cabinets; the ambitious politician's or capitalist's or general's record looked up; and, a day or two later, an amazing, amusing, or salacious, but always perfectly true, bit of gossip will appear in the newspapers.

Paris will then smile. Paris will whisper and cackle and ridicule.

And no man, whatever his strength of will and whatever the power of iron or gold at his command, can win out against the cruel, merciless wit of the boulevards. It was because of this card system and the blighting laughter which followed the exposure of certain indelicate details of his private life, that General Boulanger, instead of becoming emperor of the French, blew out his brains on the grave of his beloved mistress. It was this card system which finally wiped out the shame of the Dreyfus affair. It was this card system, even more than the heroic defence of Verdun, which cheated Emperor William the Second out of his bombastic dream of entering Paris through the Arc de Triomphe, in a conqueror's full panoply, at the head of the Prussian Guards marching in grim, serried ranks . . . .

So Poret explained.

"Many an unwritten page of history is on these little cards," he said.

And he continued:

"Stronger, this system of ours, than cannons and tanks and bombing planes. The ambitious man who thinks of conquering France should begin with destroying these bits of pasteboard." He sighed. "France is old. It is wise—and a little tired. We French abhor change, be it for better or for worse. We want neither a Mussolini nor a Lenin. We do not even care for—ah—" smiling thinly—"a Henry Ford or a J. P. Morgan—or a Rockefeller—or a William Randolph Hearst . . . ."

"Your loss—possibly?"

"Possibly!" echoed the Frenchman. "We prefer safety to glory—and bread to cake." He was silent. "And now—there were some people whom . . . .?"

"Yes—whom I'd like to have looked up."

Garth wrote down the names: Count Varolath, Colonel de Milenko, Prince Tomashin, and Sir Pascal Nahadin.

Almost he added La Sylphe. But he changed his mind.

He was curious about her. Naturally. He knew, furthermore, that, the more he found out about her, the more he would be able to help her.

He was, on the other hand, a romantic, rather quixotic young man; a Sir Lancelot—you might say—without too much naiveté. He could not bring himself to spy on the woman whom he loved.

At least, he could not spy on her directly; could

not, by including her name, tell this sardonic Frenchman:

"Here's somebody else about whom I have my doubts."

And so he handed the list to Poret who passed it on to one of the elderly clerks; while, at just about the same time, a small, freckled, impudent messenger boy entered the Club of the Failures, whistling shrilly, waving two telegrams—the ones sent, an hour or so earlier, by Garth to Tomashin and Varolath—and disturbing thereby M. Toussaint Duval, the stout, red-nosed caretaker who was pleasantly busy with his short, black pipe and the perusal of a lurid murder trial as reported in the *Petit Parisien* . . . .

CHAPTER SEVEN

TELEGRAMS for parties called. . . ."

The boy's tongue tripped over the exotic Wallachian names; and Duval took the thin, blue envelopes.

"What are you waiting for?" he demanded.

"What do you imagine I'm waiting for?"

"A tip—eh? Nothing doing, ignoble young bloodsucker!"

"Aw—" came the reply. "Kick yourself in the pants, specimen of an obese hippopotamus! And—what I know about your mother. . . ."

"Out you go, O arrogant pimple!"

And the boy made a rapid and undignified exit, propelled by a square-toed, capable, number eleven boot, almost colliding on the threshold with Malik who came in from the outside, a bandage around his forehead.

Yes—he informed Duval in answer to the latter's question—the bandage was the result of last night's taxicab accident.

"I read about it in the paper," said the other. "And Prince Tomashin. . . . ?"

"Not badly hurt. But he'll have to stay in bed for a day or two."

"Telegram arrived for him this very minute."

"Oh . . . ?"

"And one for Count Varolath."

"Keep the Count's here. He usually lunches at the club, doesn't he?"

"Yes."

"Let me have the other." He went out into the street, accompanied by Duval, and stepped into a taxicab that had drawn up. "I'll drive over to the Hotel Violette—on the Place de Thionville—and give it to the Prince. . . ."

The chauffeur heard—and laughed.

"A Prince—on the Place de Thionville?" he mocked. "Ah—citizen—you had a drop too much!"

He stepped on the gas. Nor should you blame him for his ironic incredulity since, after all, the Place de Thionville is the Place de Thionville.

You will find it—though heaven knows why you should look for it—not far from the Church of Saint-Jacques-de-Grâce. You will find it a packed, greasy, sooty wilderness—a dusky tracery of chimney-stack and gas-work—a vulgar ecstasy of gutters and garrets—a maze of brick-and-stucco tenements pierced with countless, unevenly spaced windows that are enlivened by bird cages and anæmic, potted flowers and rags hung out to dry and, if the weather is warm, by the frowzy heads of housewives greeting each other in clipped, metallic jargon—"*bonjour, la p'tite mère . . . et la santé—ça colle toujours?*"—and then some broadly Rabelaisian jest as one of the artisans looks up from his basement shop and joins in the small-talk of the women.

No verdure there except an occasional, sickly fig-tree straggling along a rusty water-pipe, or perhaps a discouraged bit of clematis or convolvulus reaching up. No beauty. No charm.

Lots of life, though—if it is the sort of life you care for.

Life in the raw; shrilling, shrieking, laughing, belching, cursing, fighting, making love. Latin life. Life gloriously free and unashamed.

And, incongruously, smack in the centre of this quite improper and rowdyish neighborhood, the quite proper and refined Hotel Violette; really a *pension* patronized by the less wealthy and more serious-minded Anglo-Saxon tourists—the sort who go in for culture and calories and Theodore Dreiser and Greek dancing and Senator Borah and modernistic furniture and prison reform and the Theatre Guild; patronized, too, by a few Eastern European aristocrats who have seen more prosperous days and have not, at least not yet, reached the gigolo stage.

Amongst them was Prince Maxime Tomashin—stretched out on a couch, his left arm in a sling; rather good-looking in a hawkish way, the sabre scar across his jaw accentuating his stark virility.

He smiled at Malik who smiled back.

"Feeling better, Prince?"

"Much better. Thanks."

Malik—who was a Syrian and whose full name was Malik el-Khoury—was the other's valet, confidential secretary, and general factotum. He had been his very shadow ever since, during the world war, the Prince, whose country had been allied to the Central Powers and Turkey and who had been sent to Constantinople on an important military mission, had saved the other from a well-deserved fate of seven years at hard labor, thereby earning his undying gratitude and devotion. Indeed—according to Tomashin's cynical and quite truthful remark—this devotion was the Syrian's one and only decent trait.

"Telegram for me?" asked Tomashin.

"Yes."

Tomashin read—and laughed.

"It's from that man last night," he explained, "that impostor who masqueraded as Karolus—telling me where he stabled my roadster. . . ."

"Impudence!"

"But such amusing impudence!"

Again Tomashin laughed. Then, quickly, he became serious.

"It is hard," he went on, "to fight in the dark—against an unknown enemy."

"I'll find out who he is. . . ."

"Sure of yourself?"

"Have I ever failed you?"

"Never."

"Nor shall I fail you today. First I'll get your car."

He left; and so, while, in the Bureau of Registry, Garth's espionage was getting under way, the counter-espionage against him was also getting under way; and it was in able hands—hairy, nervous, high-veined Syrian hands.

Malik claimed the roadster without any trouble. He took it to the garage where Tomashin usually kept it, examined it thoroughly for any scraps of evidence, and found the two things which the American had forgotten: the velvet face mask and the fur cap with the aigrette.

The face mask was similar to a hundred others. But the cap had a label with the name and address of a costumer's shop:

"Maison Josette. 117 rue Henri-Monier."

He drove there. With the help of a few francs changing hands, he learned that the cap, as part of a complete Wallachian outfit, had been sold, only a day or two earlier, to Sir Pascal Nahadin.

He smiled. Here was important information which he telephoned to Prince Tomashin.

Then he went to the Hotel Excelsior.

He did not use the front door. But he slipped into the hotel by using the back entrance—past great garbage pails spilling their acrid contents, huge trucks delivering meat and fruit and vegetables, a mound of coal waiting to be shoveled into the cellar, mysterious nests of battered tomato cans, and a line strung from pole to pole where the Alsatian chef's underwear was swinging in the breeze with that pompous and self-righteous dignity peculiar to wet, red flannel.

Always the back entrance. Always the scurrying around corners. It was the Syrian's way through life, topographically as well as psychologically.

It is easy and dangerous to overcolor and overstate, to pile high-light on high-light and shadow on shadow. But it would be almost impossible to paint Malik's character—except for his devotion to Tomashin—a richer, deeper black than it was. Perhaps it was not entirely his own fault, since he had been born and bred in the slums of Constantinople; earning his living since he was a small child, kicked and beaten and starved; later on graduating to the proud position of guide, dragoman, and all-round pimp. His own fault or not, the fact remained: he was an exaggeration in infamy and a hyperbole in knavery. He was unsavory and dishonest in a fabulous, grotesque Oriental manner. A man he was whose coiling, obscene wits were sharpened to a needle's point; wits that, thanks to a cynical and bitter knowledge of human nature, and etched on his brain a double wisdom: to help the undeserving, since they, because of fear and weakness, can be made to pay a thousandfold, and to collect scraps of miscellaneous information as a rat collects refuse.

Thus, always, in this man's life, it was the back way. Thus, today, as he slipped into the Hotel Excelsior, he asked himself:

"Whom do I know here? What do I know about whom I know? How can I use whom and what I know?"

The question was easily answered. There was, working here, a certain Kristine Karapoulos, a Greek chambermaid and a native of Constantinople.

A couple of years ago, when he had returned there on a visit, the girl's father, whom he knew, had needed help desperately. He had rendered it. Since then—frequently reminding her of her father's obligation, so as to "stimulate gratitude with the whip of dread," as he put it—he had made her pay for it over and over again; partly by taking money from her; partly, he being a sensuous man and liking her red lips and her white arms, by forcing his passion on her.

So she hated him; feared him.

He inquired where she was, was told, and found her in the pantry. She was alone, cleaning a flower vase.

When she saw him her face took on a greenish shade. Perhaps it was the reflection of the green glass vase which she was wiping. Perhaps it was the reflection of something in her soul—that part of the soul which broods over the memory of bitter things.

Yet, to his mock-polite query in her native tongue: "How do you do, my precious Greek sweetmeat?" she replied vehemently. She cried out that she was through with him; that never again did she want to see him; that now she had a lover . . . "a strong man, a sergeant in the French army, who will break your ugly head, O creature with pig's ears!"

Malik seemed nowise offended.

"And yet," he said in a purring voice, "I remember an occasion, two years ago in Constantinople, not far from the Avrat bazaar, when your father . . ."

"Oh. . . ."

"He drew steel. He killed. . . ."

"He killed the soldier in self-defence! You know he did!"

"I do. Was I not a witness to the regrettable affair? And, being your father's friend, did I not help him to get out of the country?"

"And did we not pay you? Did we not give you what money we had? Did I not give you everything—everything?"

"Including yourself, O delight! Your crimson kisses—your body so soft and generous! And yet—be pleased to consider my conscience, rejoicer of souls. Of late it has been troubling me, especially—ah—when I pass a police station. And your father . . ."

"Is in Paris—safe—since last night," she interrupted triumphantly. "And my lover . . ."

"Will break my head. So you said. Still—tell me—is there not your grandfather in Constantinople—and your grandmother—and . . ."

"What have they to do with it?"

"Nothing at all. Only—Turkey is Turkey, my pet. And your father is a Greek—a Greek who, in self-defence or not, killed a Turkish soldier. Doubtless your father's head is safe. But—I repeat—what about your grandfather's . . . ?"

Then she broke down. She sobbed, implored—and he gave a short laugh. He had her as he wanted her: submissive, supine. He advised her not to get excited; told her that, in reality, he did not demand much.

"I only want—words."

"Words . . . ?" she puzzled, hating, suspecting, fearing him with every cell in her brain.

"Nothing else. Just a little information."

"About what?"

"About a dancer called La Sylphe—who lives here. You know her?"

"I do. I am her chambermaid."

"For which praised be whatever Greek Saints you prefer! I was afraid I would have to approach another servant through you—would have to gild crooked fingers—and I am a poor man! Tell me—at what time does La Sylphe usually leave the hotel?"

"This morning she left early—half an hour ago—to attend a rehearsal."

"For which—again—praised be all sorts of Saints! Of course you have the pass key to her apartment?"

"Yes."

"Take me there."

"But—— oh . . ."

"How you misjudge me! I have no intention of stealing. All I want is a look around."

Finally the girl obeyed. She took the Syrian to the dancer's rooms. He searched them with a rapidity, a skill and thoroughness that spoke eloquently of past experience in that line. He found—and discarded as unimportant—a number of bills paid and unpaid, a number of letters from admirers male and female.

At last, tucked away into a small drawer of the writing desk as if it were something very precious, he came upon a sheet of hotel stationery on which was scrawled:

> "Garth Brent. 19 Place de Fontenoy.
> Write, telephone, wire, when you need me.
> And I'll come at once—to break a lance
> for you."

He smiled—if not like the cat that has eaten the canary, then like the one that is about to eat it.

He caressed the girl's cheek.

"Thank you, my pet," he said. "You are a pretty, dear little thing. If I were not in such a hurry today I might feel inclined to linger—and taste the perfume of your passion."

With which delicate compliment he left her; then, again using the back way, stepped out of the hotel; and hastened across town toward the Place de Fontenoy.

In the meantime, in the basement of the Bureau of Registry, Poret had given to Garth several cards with the records of Tomashin, Varolath, and de Milenko.

"Is there no card referring to Sir Pascal?" inquired the American.

"A whole nest of them. Enough to write a long biography. But . . ."

"But . . . ?"

"They are marked with a large, red cross."

"Meaning . . . ?"

"That they cannot be produced without a special permit from the Minister of Foreign Affairs."

"And, therefore, no chance for me to . . . ?"

"Not a chance in the world, I'm afraid. Some time ago the American ambassador, acting on behalf of your President, wished to consult one of these confidential *bordereaux*. And we had to refuse."

Poret went to his desk, while Garth turned to the perusal of the cards.

They were neatly typed and contained short, dry statements of fact. They related that all three men were Wallachian noblemen; that they had distinguished themselves in the military as well as the diplomatic service of their country; that they had fought in the world war and, later on, with the White counter-revolutionaries against the Reds; that they had once been intimate with the former Crown Prince Karolus; that they had turned against him at the time of his sudden abdication; that they had been amongst a group of aristocrats who, publicly, had hanged Karolus in effigy, in front of the royal palace, nailing a great placard with the single word "Traitor" to the gallows; that, after the establishment of the republic, they had been exiled and had gone to Paris where, today, they were earning a modest livelihood—Tomashin as a fencing instructor, Varolath as a riding master, and de Milenko as a teacher of languages.

It appeared, furthermore, that they had been neither better nor worse than most men of their social standing. For, in the days before revolution had sounded "taps" to their fortunes, they had gambled for high stakes. They had freely looked upon the wine when it was red—or white. For causes grave or trivial, they had fought their shares of duels which, in Tomashin's case, had twice resulted in the opponent's death. And, more to their financial than to their moral sorrow, they had kept women that had been too fast and race horses that had been too slow.

All told—considered Garth—there seemed to have been nothing in their past which, from the point of view of their corner of Continental Europe where life had not yet simmered down to the drab level of thin-blooded, middle-class Puritanism, could be construed as reflecting in any way on their honor or integrity.

Only two items impressed Garth. Both were contained in Tomashin's record.

One said:

> "There is gossip among local Wallachian aristocrats that Maxine Tomashin is the adopted son of the late Prince Gregoire Tomashin; and that he is, in reality, the illegitimate offspring of the former king's twin-brother and an Italian actress who dropped out of sight at the time when her lover entered a monastery. There is also rumor that this actress is Signora Carlotta Cuneo, the mistress of Sir Pascal Nahadin.
>
> "For additional reference consult *bordereaux* A 789236 (Cuneo) and C 557893 (Nahadin)."

The second item which interested the American—which, indeed, startled him—related:

> "Prior to Karolus' abdication, Tomashin was engaged to Princess Nadine, the former's sister and Prince Danielo's twin."

Garth put down the card. He lit a cigarette. A shadow darkened his eyes as he called to mind the curious conversation which, after the duel, in the lobby of the Club of the Failures, he had overheard between Tomashin and La Sylphe; Tomashin telling her that he had not changed, in anything, not even in his devotion to her; and, afterwards, the curt interplay of questions and answers:

"You have forgotten—everything . . . .?"

"Yes."

"You—you mean it?"

"I do, Maxime."

"There are not even memories?"

"Not even memories. . . ."

La Sylphe and Nadine—he wondered—were they one and the same? Or was La Sylphe just a little dancer who had once been the other's mistress?

The thought hurt; hurt terribly.

He was a modern man—he reminded himself—with modern sex standards; a man who all his life—rather proud of his liberal philosophy and, too, rather naif in his pride—had refused to subscribe to the bloody, cruel, ancient fetish of virginity, of pre-marital chastity. And yet—queer how, suddenly, the moment the issue was no longer academic but personal, the same old intolerant Adam peeped through, judging—and condemning—the same old Eve. Queer—and maddening—that a man's body should rule and bully his heart and soul—and his brain. Should rule it because of love—— Garth considered—the selfishness of love; the craft and malice and trickery and meanness of love. . . .

Oh yes. The meanness of love.

The meanness of wishing to be the first—always the first.

Philosophers claimed that love was largely made of curiosity. They were wrong. Love was largely made of mistrust—and possessiveness; the desire of owning all of a beautiful thing; the present, the future—and, chiefly, the past.

It was brutal. It was unreasonable. Garth knew it—and could not get away from it. . . .

La Sylphe—Tomashin's mistress. . . . ?

He shook his head.

Impossible. He would not believe it. The other thing must be true: La Sylphe and Nadine were one and the same. . . .

He was interrupted in his thoughts by Poret who had stepped up, who asked:

"How are you making out?"

"Fair to middling. By the way, I wonder if you could let me have another record. . . ."

"Signora Cuneo's? No. It's marked confidential."

Garth stared at the Frenchman.

"Mind-reader—are you?" he demanded.

"It used to be my job."

"In a circus side-show—with a pink turban around your head—and charging ten francs a throw?"

"Not exactly. It used to be my job in war time—as it was *your* job. . . ."

"Oh. . . ."

"For, doubtless, you're the same Garth Brent who, in the year 1917, when certain papers disappeared in connection with the new French poison gas. . . ."

"Was able to assist your countrymen? Yes."

Both smiled. Then Poret went on, with elaborate carelessness:

"Incidentally, I was at the ball last night—at the Club of the Failures. . . ."

"You were there—officially?"

"Quite unofficially. Showing a provincial cousin the wicked sights of Paris. A provincial cousin who was scared to death—when . . ."

"When . . . ?"

"A pistol shot was fired." Poret coughed. "By the way—is it possible, by any chance, that you were there, too?"

"I was."

"Also—unofficially?"

"Yes." Garth lowered his voice. "Unofficially—upon my honor! I'm no longer connected with the Intelligence Service of my country. Nor does America take the slightest interest in Wallachia."

"Still—you had a reason to . . . ?"

"A personal reason."

"Which means either money—or woman."

"Or both. Or—it may begin with money. . . ."

"And wind up with woman. I know," smiled Poret. "Therefore—remembering your help in the matter of the poison gas—may I—again unofficially—tell you something?"

"About . . . ?"

"Wallachia. The iron crown of Wallachia."

"Never heard of it."

"Didn't think you had. That's why I am telling you. This iron crown—and the traditions that surround it—dates back to the days, five centuries ago, when the Turks, then at the height of their military power, invaded Servia, Austria, Hungary, Silesia; when they invaded, and almost conquered, Wallachia; when the Wallachians, princes and peasants, rich and poor, sacrificed their all to stem the Moslem tide, selling jewels, precious metals, everything and anything, to buy weapons; when King Mirko the Second, the direct ancestor of Karolus, sold to a Venetian money lender the great, golden, emerald-studded crown and substituted for it one made of iron. Since those days," Poret continued, "the Wallachians have looked upon this iron crown with superstitious awe. No man can be rightfully acknowledged king unless, with his own hands, he puts it upon his head."

He paused; went on:

"Rumor has it that, at the time of Karolus' abdication, the crown disappeared—although the legitimists, the royalists, deny this rumor—insist that it is in the vaults of the Bank of England." Poret coughed. "Personally I believe that the royalists are—lying. . . ."

He was silent.

"I don't suppose," asked Garth softly, "you've any idea what the crown looks like?"

"I've seen it."

"Oh . . . ?"

"It isn't really a crown, but an iron band, amazingly flexible, and beautifully carved and chiseled."

"How thick?"

"About half the thickness of this pencil."

"Easily hidden—don't you think?" suggested the American.

"Very easily hidden. For instance—in the lining of a hat. . . ."

"A man's?"

"Why not a woman's? It might also be slipped, like a bit of whalebone, into the top seam of a veil. . . ."

"Or concealed by the elastic that holds a face mask in place?"

"Shouldn't wonder," agreed the Frenchman.

They smiled at each other.

"Thank you, M. Poret."

"Don't mention it. You see, France owes you a debt of gratitude—in the matter of the poison gas. France might owe you even more gratitude if . . ."

"If I should assist her in washing her dirty linen?"

The other flared up.

"Do you call it washing dirty linen," he demanded, "to keep the peace of Europe . . . ?"

"I beg your pardon," exclaimed Garth. "I really, contritely, beg your pardon. Again—many thanks!"

They shook hands warmly. Poret returned to his desk, while the American left the basement. He stopped at Charles de Montfort's office.

"Well," inquired the latter, "are you through with your mysterious investigations?"

"I am—for the time being."

"Find out what you were after?"

"Yes—and no. But . . ."

"But . . . ?"

"I've an idea I discovered the girl's name."

"What girl's?"

"The girl I told you about—the one I'm going to marry. . . ."

"Aren't drunk by any chance?"

"Not the least bit."

"All right—then you *need* a drink. Seven drinks. Come on. I'll take you to the nearest bistro and buy them for you—though I can ill afford it. . . ."

"Of course you can't. Which reminds me—I'll write you a check."

"Rubber check?"

"Perfectly good, honest-to-God check. I'll mail it to you today. I'm flush again."

"Eh . . . ?"

"I mean it. You see——" and Garth was thoroughly enjoying the look of incredulous amazement on his friend's face—"this morning one hundred thousand dollars were deposited to my credit . . . "

"By the Archangel Gabriel, I suppose?"

"By a multimillionaire who needed my help—and paid spot cash like a little gent."

"What do you call this? Scenario for a melodrama which—mistakenly—you expect to sell?"

"It happens to be the truth. And truth is stranger than . . ."

"Fiction. I'm familiar with the hoary bromide."

"But—truth *is* stranger than fiction, Charles. Why—I've met actresses who never once lost their jewels. I've talked to Armenians who didn't claim that their nearest and dearest had their jolly old throats cut by the unspeakable Turk. I've dined with a British Royal Highness who dropped her *h*'ches—and I've lunched with a Bowery rag-picker who explained to me all about Confucius and Einstein and the difference between the Copernican and Pythagorean systems. I've come across Scotch Jews and a Buddhist priest by the name of Sarsfield O'Shea. I've known a nun who has been an emperor's mistress—and a motion picture star who has been nobody's mistress—and I could tell you a raft of other quaint and extraordinary experiences . . ."

"But I won't let you!" cried the other, thoroughly exasperated. "I've work to do. Get out of here!"

And the American laughed. He left the Bureau of Registry.

Farther up the street he saw a small, dusty, public square. It was a typical Paris square, named after some deservedly forgotten patriot or artist; and it consisted of seventeen bedraggled chestnut trees, an enormous, battered tin receptacle for waste paper, and a stretch of sapless, discouraged-looking lawn where unlikely French children played with improbable French dogs.

There he found a bench. He sat down and began to dovetail and interweave the various data and scraps of information which he had gathered, to arrive at certain conclusions—and to make certain guesses.

Chiefly guesses.

Guessing was his way, his method. It had been his method during the world war, when he had been attached to the Military Intelligence Service; a method which some of his superior officers, while admitting and admiring the results, had called slipshod, which he personally pronounced to be applied psychology, and which might, with equal justice, be styled applied poetry.

For, although he never entirely lost sight of facts, Garth—unlike the average Frenchman to whom life is a mathematical problem constructed of algebraic formulae—would not permit these same facts to bully him, nor would he raise logic to the pedestal of an idol. Instead he progressed by leaps and bounds of his imagination, by sudden, intuitive graspings at seemingly trivial and unimportant details; occasionally leaving loose threads which he would pick up later on and tie into place, whenever he had the chance, and calmly forgetting all about them if the chance did not happen to arise.

There had been, for instance, the poison gas affair of which Poret had reminded him.

The French authorities had been unable to trace the traitor who had purloined—and, doubtless, stolen—the secret. They had been at their wits' ends. Then, on Charles de Montfort's advice, Garth had been called in on the case, and had presently pointed the finger of suspicion at Dr. Toussaint Guizot, a civilian scientist in the Department of Chemical Warfare.

General Marmont, in charge of the investigation, had scoffed.

Guizot—a traitor . . . ? Toussaint Guizot, that dapper, neat, almost foppish little man—and so hard-working, so meticulous and conscientious. . . ."

"Out of the question!" General Marmont had exclaimed.

"And yet I've got a hunch."

"Oh . . ."

"Ever notice his bowler hat, General?"

"What about it? It's a very ordinary bowler hat."

"But—it's always dusty."

"What does that prove?"

"I don't know—but I wonder. You see—the rest of the man is so neat, so exceedingly well washed and well brushed. Why isn't his hat? There must be a reason. And I tell you what I think this reason is. . . ."

"Well . . . ?"

"Something's weighing on his mind."

"Quite possible. Perhaps his mistress has deceived him."

"Or perhaps *he* has deceived—his fatherland."

"Fantastic, grotesque Yankee bizarrerie!" General Marmont had snorted.

But he had followed Garth's lead—with the result that, two weeks later, Dr. Guizot had suffered the supreme, tragic humiliation of facing, blindfolded, a firing squad of twelve riflemen; and with the further result that another medal had joined the many on Garth's chest and that the General had said to him:

"This is your moment to flap your wings and crow. And still—it can't be so . . . ."

"Reminds me of the hick," had been the American's laughing rejoinder, "who, for the first time in his life, sees a giraffe and exclaims: 'There ain't no such animal!' "

"Something like it. You see—to suspect a man because his hat is dusty . . . . ah—" Marmont's logical French soul had writhed at the idea—"how preposterous! How utterly inconsistent!"

"Maybe," Charles de Montfort had commented, "Garth is too clever to be afraid of inconsistencies . . . ."

A remark meant in friendly irony. Yet a remark which spoke the truth.

For Garth Brent was clever, in the quick, pouncing, careless American way that did not mind putting the cart before the horse, if it happened to serve the purpose. On the other hand—perhaps because he belonged to a young and rather cruel race which takes a delight in pricking bubbles—he was a little ashamed of his own cleverness; and it was for this reason that, frequently, he hid it behind a smoke screen of light, jesting flippancy.

So here he sat now, on the bench in the small, public square; and he watched the spindle-shanked, overdressed children and the clipped poodles and the beribboned Breton nursemaids; and he wondered and puzzled and concluded and guessed; and, presently, he blended conclusions and guesses into a story.

A story—he thought—which, given the involved political situation on which it was based, was dry and drab and prosy enough to please the most matter-of-fact editorial writer.

Yet a story that held the echoes of sounding brass and tinkling cymbals—the tragic, discordant cymbals of a regal pomp that had been swept away by the maelstrom of war and revolution and that would never be seen again. A story tinted with the gold of pride and the gold of passion. A story that spoke of cups once filled with wine, filled today with the bitter dregs of remembrance; that spoke, no less, of a great love uplifted like a lily before the Lord God. . . .

CHAPTER EIGHT

MANY years ago—so this prosy, tragic story related—Prince Breda of Wallachia, twin-brother to the reigning monarch, was banished to a monastery because, an ardent, hot-headed youth, deeply in love with Carlotta Cuneo, an Italian actress, he resented the king's interference in this affair and rashly threatened armed rebellion. Shortly afterwards, his mistress gave birth to a son who was adopted by Prince Gregoire Tomashin; and though Garth figured out the reasons for this adoption—dynastic reasons, a deliberate blotting out of the child's identity lest, after he grew up to manhood, he should carry on his father's feud—he did not understand how the woman had been persuaded or forced to submit to giving up her son.

Then, more than two decades later, the world war broke out. Russian troops invaded Wallachia. The monastery was bombarded. In the turmoil and confusion Breda escaped; and, using the name of Pascal Nahadin and backed by a gigantic fortune of mysterious origin, he appeared in Paris. There, immediately and actively, he favored the cause of the Allied

Powers, although his native land was fighting on the side of Germany.

In Paris, once more, Carlotta Cuneo came to him. Once more—as if the long, intervening years of separation and Trappist silence had not existed—they became lovers. Once more they relived their ancient passion—so strange and so high—so ludicrous given their age—and so much wiser and finer than the whirl of sceptic moths and cynical butterflies that was all about them.

Was their illegitimate child, Maxime Tomashin, aware of the secret and shame of his birth? Had, perhaps, his parents let him know who he was . . . ?

Garth doubted it.

He pictured, instead, Sir Pascal and Carlotta Cuneo watching their son from afar throughout the grim duration of the war; watching, with anxiety and, too, with pride, his brilliant career in the military and diplomatic service of Wallachia until, finally, he became engaged to Nadine and was foremost amongst the adherents and intimate friends of Crown Prince Karolus.

But defeat came. Revolution came—bringing the new freedom, harsh and brave and clamorous as a trumpet blast; bringing a clean light of scorn for dusty, worn-out Gothic feudalism. There was democracy's ruthless, bloody gesture: the murder of King Mirko.

Even so, all was not lost. Karolus might have

mounted the throne. He might have appealed to arms with fair hope of success. And then, on the eve of his coronation, he abdicated.

The reason . . . ?

A quite ordinary, quite human reason—Garth answered his own question.

It was simply that, suddenly, faced with the grave responsibilities of kingship, there had died in Karolus the lust for power and pomp, for glory and dominion. He had become tired of strife; tired of seeing his fatherland torn and trampled on and crucified; tired of greasing the wheel of personal ambition with the blood of his countrymen; tired of ruling peasants and poor for the sake and benefit of lords and lackeys.

Ah—there was neither comfort nor decency in such a victory.

At all events—prompted by conscience or boredom or, possibly, a blending of both—he abdicated. At once, with chilly, hard violence, with hatred as plain and honest as bread and salt, Tomashin turned against him. And the engagement with Nadine was broken off. For she was devoted to her older brother. She agreed with him; saw eye to eye with him.

His kingly occupation gone, Karolus left the country. Danielo disappeared; Nadine did likewise; while Tomashin and the other irreconcilable aristocrats emigrated, biding their time until the coming of age of Prince Danielo who, unlike his brother and sister, was hand-in-glove with the royalists.

Karolus knew that the latter would move heaven and earth to obtain possession of the iron crown without which none could rightfully be acknowledged King of Wallachia. He knew, too, that he would be unable to protect it with his own person.

He wondered what to do.

Should he deposit it with a bank. The Bank of England or the Bank of France?

Not safe enough. Due to Karolus' abdication, Danielo was now heir to the throne. He would bring legal proceedings against the bank; would force the surrender of the crown.

There was only one safe place. Nadine. Karolus entrusted the crown to her. It was because of this crown that Nadine, grown famous in Paris as La Sylphe, wore veil or mask wherever she went—slipping the narrow, flexible metal band into the top seam of her veil, or concealing it by the elastic that held her face mask in position; mask and veil cloaking her features and her identity no less than they cloaked the ancient, sacred symbol of sovereignty.

Not only that—thought Garth. His imagination leaped on.

It told him that Nadine's very profession had been chosen with clever care. For, thanks to the sensational publicity caused by mask and veil, she was always in the public eye; and this was yet another safeguard—for her as well as for the iron crown.

A week from Saturday Danielo would come of age.

On that day, should he enter the capital and claim his royal inheritance, there would be again revolution and bloodshed, men herded and slaughtered in wrath, the drums and the guns crashing out their waltz of death.

To this Sir Pascal had referred when he had said to Garth that tragedy was a conflict between right and right; meaning a conflict between the two opposing principles, both sincerely held, of republicanism and monarchism. Sir Pascal was a republican and a pacifist; had, doubtless, for this reason helped the Allied Powers during the war. But Maxime Tomashin, his illegitimate son, had different views. He was the sort of die-hard aristocrat who, deep in his medieval soul, believed in the right of the bright sword, who believed in the swaggering, arrogant pride of spear and golden spur and crested helmet and escutcheon with twenty-four quarterings.

This man, this king-maker, was determined that Danielo should mount the throne. And he knew where Danielo was . . . a fact borne out by his remark to the American, after the duel:

"Your spies are clever. But—you didn't find him after all—did you?"

Tomashin had marked out a careful course of action. Somehow, he had pierced La Sylphe's secret; had detected that she was Nadine and that she had the iron crown of Wallachia in her keeping, taking it along wherever she went, concealing it by veil or mask. Through the Club of the Failures he had tendered her an invitation to appear there as a paid performer; with the purpose of creating a scene, of demanding that she should remove her mask, and then, when she refused, of ripping it off and, in the confusion which was bound to ensue, of making away with it—and with the crown.

Curiously, this plan dovetailed with the counterplan of Sir Pascal who had got wind of part, at least, of the monarchist plot.

Acting in concert with Karolus and Nadine and hearing of the invitation, he had asked her to accept, to go. Not alone, though. Karolus, too, should be there. For Sir Pascal had figured out that the club would be the safest and most logical place of refuge for Danielo; he would be amongst staunch adherents who would guard him with their lives. It was possible that Karolus and Nadine might run across him there; or, perhaps, Danielo might obey the call of the blood, the call of sentiment, and talk to them, thereby giving them the chance to argue with him about the royalist intrigues, to try to dissuade him.

But plan and counterplan had miscarried.

Karolus' airplane had crashed, landing him in the Lyons hospital. Sir Pascal, aware that Nadine would be alone and in danger, had been at his wits' end what to do and had sent the American to her rescue. And the American had succeeded. He had protected Nadine; had, by the same token, defeated Tomashin—if only for the time being.

For there was the latter's remark:

"The game is not over yet. Doubtless—soon—we'll play another round. . . ."

Here, then, was this story as Garth told it to himself. It seemed quite plausible, quite tightly knit, except for a few points that bothered him.

Why, knowing that Karolus had been disabled, had not Sir Pascal sent word to Nadine, asking her not to go to the club that night?

Why, since she, too, had had news of the accident, had she gone there, even without receiving word from Sir Pascal?

How had Tomashin discovered her double secret—the secret of her identity and the secret that the iron crown was in her possession?

Why had he assured her that, in snatching at her mask, his sole intention had been to force a quarrel on the man whom he had imagined to be Karolus?

Garth speculated, advanced reasons, discarded them, and found an answer to one question only—the last.

Given the superstitious awe with which the Wallachian peasants, the people least touched by the spirit of democracy, regarded the ancient, sacred symbol of sovereignty, it was on the cards that Tomashin would make another attempt—and yet another—to get it into his hands. Naturally he had not wished

Nadine to suspect his knowing that she was the crown's guardian; had not wished to forewarn and forearm her; had, therefore, told her an untruth.

Yes—thought Garth—that was it.

But he was unable to answer the other questions; decided there was just one way of finding out.

He would go to Sir Pascal; would say to him straight:

"Look here! I'm in this mystery. I know a good deal about it—but not everything. I love La Sylphe—Nadine—your niece, isn't she? Well—I want to help her—and you—and Karolus. Tell me the whole truth. Let's work together."

He rose. He consulted the telephone directory in a nearby tobacconist's shop to find out Sir Pascal's business address; hailed a taxicab; and had himself driven to No. 79 rue du Quatre-Septembre.

There, in an outer office immensely and depressingly respectable with shiny mahogany, Axminster rugs, red leather, and steel engravings in heavy gilt frames, he was surprised to see Dennis Courvoisier—a Franco-American whom he had known at Harvard and whom he had met again in the mud of the trenches.

They had never been friends. They might have been enemies, had their acquaintanceship been less casual. Courvoisier had always objected to Garth's flippancy and had, besides, envied his higher social standing. And Garth had always poked fun at Courvoisier's lugubrious seriousness, at his doleful and grim determination to forge ahead, at his mind, as prosy as a problem in abstract dynamics, in which all the accepted standards and proper prejudices stood in a solemn row, neatly marshaled and labeled and holding each other by the hand.

"Well," exclaimed Garth, "what are *you* doing here?"

"I am Sir Pascal's private secretary."

"You *would* be—somebody's secretary!"

An unkind remark; but true enough.

Indeed—hook-nosed, horse-faced, wearing his braided morning-coat, his white carnation boutonniere, and his horn-rimmed spectacles as if they were the sacramental vestments of some pompous, pagan faith of which he was high-priest—Dennis Courvoisier would have been the ideal confidential factotum for any Mumbo-Jumbo rich and important enough to need one. For he was suave, but firm, obsequious but inexorable. He knew how to handle the importunate seeker after patronage or market tips; the reporter sent out to get an indiscreet statement or to steal an indiscreet snapshot; the politician soliciting party funds; the professor of economics armed with a nostrum guaranteed to cure all financial and commercial ills; the great, official panjandrum with a well-stored mind badly arranged; the personal friend who imagines that everyone has the same amount of leisure as himself; the adventuress ready for adultery or blackmail or both. He knew how to speed them on their way, one and all, without either interview or grievance.

He walked up to Garth and gave him a limp hand to shake.

"I suppose," he asked, "you wish to see the chief."

"Right."

The other smiled, a little patronizingly, a little meanly; and Garth went on:

"What makes you look like that?"

"Like what?"

"The way you do. Sort of—how shall I put it?—oh—guilty as well as licking your chops. Rather like the sporting church elder who's about to elope with the pretty choir singer. . . ."

"I never cared much for your brand of humor."

"Too bad. Anyway—tell Sir Pascal. . . ."

"He's not in to anybody."

"I know that line of bunk. Multimillionaire. Big shot. In conference. Tell him just the same . . ."

"No use." Again Courvoisier smiled. "He is—chiefly—not in to you."

"Eh . . . ?"

"Sir Pascal's orders."

"Oh—bolony!"

"His orders," insisted the other. "He refuses to see you—today—or tomorrow—or any other time. Is that quite clear, my dear Brent?"

Garth made for a door marked "private."

"I'm going to find out how big a liar you are," he announced.

"Oh—but you mustn't . . ."

"Get out of my way!"

And he brushed Courvoisier aside, opened the door, and entered the inner office.

Sir Pascal was at his desk. He sat there, sunk into himself, numb, inert, torpid, the skin on his throat hanging loose and flabby. It was as if, since the preceding night, he had aged by twenty years.

Garth was surprised. He was shocked; was conscious of a deep, driving, almost tender pity for the man.

Then, the next moment, his pity disappeared as the other looked up, saw him, and put him on the defensive with his first words:

"Why are you here? I gave orders to . . ."

"I know," interrupted the American. "But—I'd like to speak to you."

"The desire is not mutual."

Garth drew himself up.

"Pardon?" he demanded stiffly.

"The desire is not mutual," repeated the financier. "I paid you—didn't I?—paid you well. Still—you fought a duel. You risked your life . . ."

"Oh—you have heard. . . . ?"

"Yes. Therefore, if you want more money, I'll write you another check."

Garth winced. He stared at the older man in

silence for a while, with a heated face in which there hung a red shadow of anger. He was on the point of answering rudeness with violent rudeness.

Then, with a hard effort, he brought his temper under control.

It was not—he considered—as if he gave a tinker's curse for Sir Pascal, or for Wallachia, or for all this play and counterplay of coiling, political intrigues. He was an American. His national, nationally selfish, interest lay beyond the Atlantic. Europe—the whole of it—had never touched his affections. It meant nothing to him except a place where a man of leisure might spend this same leisure rather charmingly, where hypocrisy was cut down to a pleasant minimum, where morals were not so fine and wire-drawn as to be uncomfortable, where the food was less pure but more tasty, and where one could get a decent bottle of Montrachet 1914—that sunny, golden, perfumed vintage—for a reasonable price.

No. Wallachia—Europe—meant nothing in his life.

But there was the girl whom he loved. Her fate seemed entangled in that of Wallachia. She was in trouble, needed help. . . .

He turned to Sir Pascal.

"You paid me generously," he admitted. "Too generously. . . ."

"Then . . . ?"

"Permit me to have my say. I'm not here to get

more money out of you. In fact—" the Don Quixote in him popping suddenly, gloriously, carelessly, to the surface—"I'll give you back your money! To hell with the lousy lot of it!"

He slammed the desk with his fist; again remembered La Sylphe; added more quietly:

"I came here, solely, to offer my assistance."

"Your assistance is not needed. Indeed, I resent your interference."

Here were churlish, ungracious words . . . and the red anger returned to Garth; swayed, perilously, toward red rage; presently gave way to astonishment.

Why—he—wondered—what had he done . . . ?

He voiced his wonder.

"I'll clear out all right," he declared, "nor shall I bother you again—since, evidently, I'm as unwelcome here as a safety razor salesman at a barbers' convention. Still—mere, idle curiosity—tell me—what precisely have I done to deserve such treatment?"

For a minute or two, Sir Pascal did not reply.

Then he rose. He walked up to the American and put trembling hands on his shoulders.

"Forgive me!" he muttered.

Garth, quickly roused, was quickly mollified.

"There's nothing to forgive. . . ."

"You are young—and magnanimous. There is a great deal to forgive. I was unjust, unfair. I—perhaps because I'm unhappy, so unhappy—I behaved like a cad."

"Forget it!"

"I repeat—you are young and magnanimous. As to the money—" and a rapid, strange quirk of humor wrinkled Sir Pascal's lips— "you've more than earned it. Don't be a romantic fool! Keep the money. . . ."

"I'll do nothing of the sort."

"You must—to prove that you've really forgiven me. Will you do it?"

Garth gave a little laugh.

"Gladly."

After a pause, he added:

"Sir Pascal—let me help you. . . ."

"You can help me one way."

"How . . . ?" eagerly.

"By dismissing from your mind, as much as you can, the drama in which last night you played a part. By not trying to delve, to dig, to inquire. Go your own way—and let me go mine."

Garth hesitated. Should he tell the other that he was in love with La Sylphe . . . ?

He decided not to. Instead he said again:

"Let me help you. I'd like to. I mean it."

"I know you do. And I am grateful. But—what can you do?"

"I spent quite a while in the Military Intelligence Service of my country. Made a fair enough record. Give me a few facts for a starter, a few names, a few dates—and I'll guarantee to get you the truth—the whole truth—and nothing but the truth."

Sir Pascal laughed. It was a sharp, thin laugh.

"The truth?" he echoed. "Oh—it's the one thing I do not wish to know."

"Why?"

"I'm afraid of it." His voice dropped a whispered octave. "There are moments in a man's life when the truth is more terrible, more wicked and heart-breaking than a dozen stark lies. . . ."

He stared at Garth.

"Years ago," he continued, "I had—ah—occasion to spend some time in a monastery, among saintly monks. And I remember one of them—a very old and very wise man—who said to me that, often, truth is an invention and snare of the Devil—an evil and accursed thing—a thing of black magic—as poisonous as a hundred snakes—and roaring like the Apocalypse. . . ."

He was silent; and Garth gave an involuntary little shudder.

He was not superstitious. But, at that moment, he felt—something. Something unearthly. Something haunting and brooding. Something like an ancient, tragic ghost that swept through the room on gray wings . . .

Then, again, he heard the other's voice.

"I suppose," the financier was asking, with a complete and startling change of tone, once more the careless man of the world, "that I'll see you at the Club Cosmopolite one of these evenings . . . ?"

Garth followed the other's cue.

"I'm looking forward to it," he replied with matter-of-fact politeness.

"I'll be glad to make a fourth at bridge — any time."

"I can't afford your stakes—a thousand francs a point, I imagine. . . . ?"

"Your credit is as excellent as your game. Au revoir, Mr. Brent."

"Au revoir, Sir Pascal."

They bowed to each other; and Garth went back into the outer office.

"I interviewed the big chief after all, didn't I?" he said to Dennis Courvoisier. "And—you noticed—he didn't kick me out on my ear."

"Yes," came the grudging admission. "You were in there nearly twenty minutes."

"I see," laughed Garth. "Keeping tabs on me, Mr. Pinkerton. And I guess you'd give your boots to know what Sir Pascal and I have been talking about . . . ? All right. I'll be a sport and put you wise. We made a bridge date." He waved a hand. "So long!"

He took a step toward the door. But the other stopped him.

"Brent!"

"Yes . . . ?"

"I want to tell you something."

"Go right ahead."

"If I were you, I wouldn't . . ."

"Wouldn't what . . . ?"

"Wouldn't monkey with the buzz-saw."

Courvoisier had spoken in a low voice; and, mockingly, Garth followed suit.

"Why the fog-signal?" he demanded in thick, stagey accents. "Why the yellow flag—the red light—the grim alarm . . . ?"

"After all, we went to college together. . . ."

"And so—for the sake of the 'rah-rah-rah!' bunk, the 'die-for-dear-old-whooziz!'—you're slipping me a bit of friendly warning . . . ?"

"That's it."

Garth shook his head.

"What you need," he commented, "is a twisted snaffle in that mouth of yours."

Courvoisier seemed annoyed as well as puzzled; and the other hastened to explain:

"A snaffle to keep you from opening your mouth too wide—and telling whoppers, like a bad little boy. You and I never embraced and kissed and exchanged love tokens and swapped vows of eternal devotion. Our antipathy is mutual. Therefore, if you warn me, it's not because of friendship—but because . . ."

"Well . . . ?" sharply.

"I'm not sure yet, my lad. But I've got one peach of a hunch."

"It might be safer to forget your hunch."

"More John Barrymore histrionics?"

"No. A hard fact. Why should you interfere?" Courvoisier hesitated; then made up his mind and went on: "You have your hundred thousand dollars . . ."

"Oh—admitting your knowledge that I have the money—and, perhaps, the reason why I have it . . . ?"

"Never mind. Only—take my tip. Leave well enough alone. What about the Riviera, Brent?"

"I bite. What about it?"

"It's lovely down there this time of a year. San Remo—you know—Monte Carlo—the Corniche . . . the Blue Train leaves around three in the afternoon . . ."

"Maybe you're right at that."

Garth left. He turned down the street.

A shrewd suspicion and guess crossed his mind. He acted on both immediately; entered the nearest telephone booth; and demanded:

"Wagram 6408."

Presently he was connected with the Bureau of Registry, with M. Poret at the other end of the wire.

Their conversation was short.

"Look here, Poret! Remember what we talked of a while back—Wallachia, you know. . . ."

"Talked of—unofficially."

"Quite unofficially. Ever hear of a man by name of Dennis Courvoisier?"

"Sir Pascal Nahadin's private secretary?"

"The same. Is he what the Jews would call *kosher*—or the opposite?"

"I don't know."

"Mind consulting your cunning little cards?"

"I'll take a look. Will you wait?"

"Haven't the time now. I'll 'phone you again."

"Putting me to work, aren't you?"

"It was you yourself who suggested that France might not be ungrateful . . ."

"Of course," laughed Poret, "unofficially."

"Right. I know the patter. I won't charge your beloved France a single centime—won't even try for the Legion of Honor. I've enough comic ribbons now."

And he clicked down the receiver and, still obeying impulse of suspicion and guess, hurried to Sir Pascal's palace and asked for Signora Cuneo.

She joined him a few moments later, and he looked at her with a new, eager interest.

She was to him no longer a queer, elderly man's prosy, elderly mistress; but a figure of amazing romance, fantastic melodrama: her lover a king's twin-brother who had rebelled, had been banished to a monastery; her illegitimate son taken away from her, perhaps by force; and this son, today, an antagonist of his own father. A life as wild and strange and incredible as an old wives' tale—he thought—and he saw in her ravaged face the memory of great beauty and great passion.

Beauty in her hands that were still slender, white, appealing; her eyes, black eyes, burnt-out, tragic eyes, eyes that had seen things honey-sweet and things gall-bitter; her voice that held a bronze quality, like the tolling of a bell, as she said to him:

"Sir Pascal is not at home. You will find him in his office."

"I did not come here to see Sir Pascal."

"Oh . . . ?"

"I came to see *you.*"

"Me . . . ?"

"Yes, Signora."

"But,"—she seemed startled, a little frightened—"there can be no reason why you should wish to see *me.*"

"There is a reason. A perfectly good one." He watched her closely. "I suppose," he went on, "you heard about my duel last night?"

"Why should I know? I know nothing, nothing, nothing!" she exclaimed.

By the very violence of her denial he knew that she was lying; and he steeled his will for his next words:

"It wasn't really a duel. You see, the man whom I fought—Prince Tomashin—tried to murder me when he discovered that I was the better swordsman."

He felt sorry for the woman. But he could not help

it. He wanted to make sure if he was right in his belief that Signora Cuneo was Tomashin's mother. And, a second later, he was quite sure. For a spasm of pain crossed her face; and she spoke in a tense, hurt whisper:

"You must forgive Maxime. He is—in spite of what happened—a great gentleman."

Garth bowed.

"Naturally," he replied, "considering who his parents are. . . ."

She caught her breath sharply. Her hands were like fluttering gulls.

"Oh," she gasped, "you—you *know?*"

"I know—something. I guess—something. And I would like to know—everything."

She pulled herself together.

"Why should you want to know?" she demanded; and her accents were now curt and brittle and antagonistic. "Curiosity, I suppose?"

"No."

"Oh. . . . I see . . ." with cutting insult, "blackmail, eh . . . ?"

"Nor blackmail."

"What is it then . . . ?"

For a moment or two he did not answer. He looked at her consideringly, wonderingly.

Here—he thought—was a woman who had greatly loved; a woman whose love had blossomed in clear faith, hot passion, cold courage, surviving both happiness and unhappiness. Perhaps she would understand another's love and sympathize with it. Perhaps she would help him if he told her straight out about himself and La Sylphe.

He doubted that he would succceed. For he remembered Sir Pascal's bitter remark that he was afraid of learning the truth. And Garth suspected—as did Sir Pascal—what this truth was. He suspected, by the same token, Carlotta Cuneo.

Well—he decided—here, besides the off-chance of making her his friend, his ally, was one way of finding out if his suspicion was justified or not; and so he said to her:

"Last night, at the Club of the Failures, I met a girl. Call her La Sylphe. . . ."

"Or, since you know so much, Princess Nadine. Of what interest is she to me?"

"Perhaps not to you," he smiled. "But to me. You see—I love her. And she is unhappy, in trouble —I want to help her—and so I came to you to . . ."

"Stop right there!" she interrupted.

She faced him; stared at him.

"Ah," she cried shrilly; and he was utterly taken aback by the violence of her words—"what do *I* care about you—and your love? What do *I* care if Nadine is unhappy and in trouble? I—by the blessed Madonna—I hate her—hate her—hate her!"

Garth was amazed.

"You," he echoed, "you *hate* her . . . ?"

"I do! I hate her—and hers!"

"But—why . . . ?"

"Why? Why? You ask me why . . . ? Tell me! Was it not her father who took my lover out of my life and banished him to a monastery? Was it not her father who, by threatening death to Pascal unless I obeyed, made me give oath that never—even though he should escape—would I marry my lover? Was it not her father who, using that same threat, forced me to give up my son, afraid lest some day he should carry on the feud against the dynasty . . . ?"

She smiled thinly, mirthlessly.

"Not that, today, I mind having given him up," she went on. "He does not know his real parentage—and I—I am glad of it. If he knew—oh—the disgrace, the shame of his birth—it would kill him. . . ."

She paused; then spoke with harsh, solemn violence:

"Cursed be her father's memory!"

"Her father is dead."

"My hate is not dead—will never die."

She stood there, tragic, superb. Her eyes were blazing and magnificent. And Garth, watching her, was moved profoundly by this display of raw Italian passion.

Then an idea came to him; and when she pointed at the door and bade him go, he shook his head.

He was sorry for her. He was conscious of deep pity and sympathy. But there was La Sylphe. He could not let this woman's hate hurt the girl whom he loved.

"Signora," he said, "I should never have asked you for your help in this matter. You and I—we cannot be friends. Nor do I blame you for what you have done—or Tomashin—with the assistance, unless I am very much mistaken, of Dennis Courvoisier. But—there is the future. In the future"—and his voice rose menacingly—"you will do nothing, Signora . . ."

She seemed a little puzzled, a little uneasy.

"Nothing . . . ?" she questioned.

"Nothing, I mean, about—ah—Wallachian politics. You will neither plot nor intrigue. You will not help Sir Pascal's enemies—your lover's enemies," he emphasized rather brutally.

She winced.

"What makes you so sure I won't?" she demanded.

"Because there is your son. The haughty aristocrat—eh . . . ? Did you not say he would die of shame were he to find out that he's illegitimate? And I—I assure you—I shall let him know unless . . ."

"You—you cannot mean it?"

"I do."

"No, no!"

She rushed up to him. She gripped his wrists so tightly that the imprint of her fingers was visible. But he was adamant.

"I swear I shall let him know—unless you do as I

tell you. You love? Do you? So do I love! You hate? So can I hate—and hurt!"

A look of harrowing conflict, of intense suffering came into the woman's eyes. And again Garth was sorry; felt deeply moved. But the cruel task must be carried through—and he said slowly, inexorably:

"I mean it, Signora."

At last she gave in.

"You win," she whispered.

And then she broke down. She cried. She cried with high-pitched, ludicrous sobs; and he took her in his arms; he kissed her very gently; he left.

A victory—he thought—a victory without glory or gold or triumphant laughter. . . .

He walked out of the palace. He wondered what had happened at his home during his absence, if perhaps—a hope and wish more than an expectation—La Sylphe had sent him a message. And so he turned in the direction of the Place de Fontenoy where, in the meantime Malik, Tomashin's Syrian servant, had arrived and saw, on a bench in front of No. 19, the janitress enjoying the warm May sun and stroking an enormous, purring, black tomcat.

CHAPTER NINE

MADAME ERNESTINE ROSSIGNOL was the janitress' name. She was a pleasant lady of massively rounded proportions who, long since, had given up worrying about the sprouting, gray hair on upper lip and chin. A garrulous, jovial, full-blooded lady she was, fond of a glass of red wine, fond, too, of a crack of gossip and harmless scandal, always ready to pass the time of day with the first comer.

Malik stopped and raised his hat politely. She smiled at him. He smiled back.

"How d'ye do, Madame?"

"How d'ye do, Monsieur?"

"You are—pardon—the janitress?"

"At your service. Are you looking for an apartment, Monsieur?"

"Yes."

"There's one for rent. An apartment of the most elegant, the most exquisite. In fact—imagine the luxury—it contains a bath tub."

"Ah—the world is progressing."

"It is."

"Tell me, Madame—what sort of tenants . . . ?"

"Only the best. The most respectable. Not a single little cocotte . . ."

"You are strict?"

"Not too strict," she assured him hurriedly. "I am not a black-mouthed, blue-nosed Huguenot. I am not narrow-minded. I, too, have been young . . ."

"*Have* been? You *are*, Madam!"

"Flatterer! Anyway—live and let live, is my motto."

"An excellent one!"

"Therefore, if the gentlemen who live here wish to bring their little friends to spend the day . . ."

"Or, perhaps, the night . . . ?"

"Precisely. What of it? The good Lord, after all, has given soft breasts to women and strong loins to men for just one reason."

"A sound philosophy."

"Still—no little cocotte actually lives here. Because of the good priest, Father Duvergnois, who has the back apartment on the top floor. There is also a retired captain of cavalry—and a professor of mathematics . . . *chic*, don't you think?"

"Very *chic*. Any foreigners?"

"One. An American. Garth Brent by name. A droll, jaw-breaking name—*hein?* But he is charming—generous—and so gay. Always on the go. Always rushing off to parties. Why—for instance last night—a fancy dress party. He came home early this morning."

"Is that so. Dressed as a Pierrot, I suppose?"

"No. Dressed as some sort of Cossack. I saw him. His overcoat was flaring wide open. I caught a glimpse of a cherry-red tunic."

She paused; went on:

"And now—if you care to inspect the apartment . . ."

"Tomorrow. I'm in a hurry today. Many thanks—and au revoir, Madame!"

"Au revoir, Monsieur!"

And she smiled at Malik—who, again, smiled back; who walked away and failed to see Garth stepping, at that moment, out of a taxicab.

Garth, on the other hand, saw the Syrian—and drew a rapid conclusion. Too much of a coincidence—he considered—to assume that Malik just happened to be in this neighborhood. The man must have come for reasons. Nor did the American trust these reasons.

A few words with the janitress convinced him that he was right.

For, in answer to his question if, a few seconds earlier, he had not noticed her in conversation with a short, swarthy foreigner, she admitted it. She said:

"Such a charming man! He inquired about an apartment in our house."

"I've an idea I know him."

"He didn't seem to know *you*."

"Really . . . .?"

"Yes." She shrugged her shoulders. "You know how it is. One talks . . . ."

"Of course. And . . . .?"

"I happened to mention your name—happened to mention that you went to the ball last night, dressed as a Cossack—that you live here . . . ."

"Well—" said Garth, rapidly reflecting that distance meant safety—"I shan't live here much longer."

Madame Rossignol was surprised and genuinely sorry.

"Oh—" she demanded—"you are leaving Paris?"

"Yes."

"For good? You will give up the apartment?"

"No, no. I'll only be away a few weeks."

"A little vacation?"

"Exactly. Taking a run down to the Riviera," he replied, recalling Dennis Courvoisier's suggestion and eagerly jumping at it.

For he told himself that, doubtless, Tomashin and Malik were in communication with Courvoisier; that, as doubtless, the latter would report to the other two the gist of his talk with Garth. One of the three would pay him a visit—to argue or to try to bribe him or, perhaps, to use force. Now, learning from Madame Rossignol that he had gone South, they would imagine that he had taken Courvoisier's advice, that he had decided to leave well enough alone, to cease interfering in the affairs of Wallachia. It was as good a way as any of drawing a red herring across his trail.

So he added:

"I'm taking the Blue Train—this afternoon. Will you look after my rooms?"

"Gladly," she smiled. "And—your address . . . .?"

"Don't bother. I want a real vacation—I want to escape all bills . . . ."

"And all *billets-doux*—eh . . . .?"

"Right!"

He went upstairs.

"Anything happen while I was gone?" he asked George.

"No, suh. Nothin' at all."

"Throw some of my things in a bag. I'm going to the Riviera." He winked broadly. "To the Riviera—that is—officially—between you and me and the lamp post. In reality I'll be within hailing of the boulevards—going to find me a discreet little hide-out . . . ."

George looked at him reproachfully.

"I reckon I knows wot you mean, Cap. Hide-out—sho' enough—hide-out from some o' dem hussies . . . ."

Garth laughed.

"Have it your own way. You're just a brunette edition of my uncle, the Bishop. Always so—oh—so objectionable in your damned self-righteousness. Always looking for the worst motive in the other fellow. At all events, I want you to keep as mum as a tongue-tied clam with the hiccoughs—if you get what I mean.

And should any stranger come snooping round here, you tell him that I'm catching the Blue Train for Monte Carlo—that is, of course, provided the high moral standards taught you by the First African-Baptist Church of Mobile, Alabam', permit you to tell a lie."

He turned to the door.

"Pack my things," he ordered. "Stay here till you hear from me. I'll give you a ring as soon as I'm located—and then you can join me."

He left the house. Recalling the maxim of modern warfare that quick transportation is half the battle, he went to the nearest automobile dealer. There he found and bought a small, smart, fast American roadster and drove off, hunting for a place to live in.

Not in Paris itself. But—for the sake of greater safety—in the suburbs.

Finally he decided on Marly-le-Roi.

He knew it well. It was a small country town, within easy distance of the boulevards, where, half a year or so ago, he had spent a very amusing if not precisely legitimate honeymoon.

What had been the girl's name . . . .?

Lucile . . . .?

No, no. Lucile was the red-headed Belgian vaudeville actress who, afterwards, had become respectable and had married Alfredo de Sousa—that rather awful Brazilian coffee millionaire with the diamonds in his teeth who usually breakfasted off a gin-and-bitters, two green olives, and a large corona-corona.

Must have been Suzette. Yes. That was it. Delightful little Suzette Langlois of the Folies Bergère. Suzette with the bobbed, black locks, the pointed breasts, and the golden eyes.

He remembered her. He remembered that first night with her at Marly-le-Roi . . . . and how he had wondered why any human being could be so amazingly lovely; had wondered why her throat came to be so soft and white; had wondered why her curly hair smelled like rain on new-mown hay; had wondered why—oh . . . .

Suddenly, with a guilty start, he thought of La Sylphe—and forgot Suzette.

La Sylphe—mattered. She was to him the ultimate woman, the only woman.

As to the other women who had flitted in and out of his life—wasn't it Kipling who, in one of his poems, had written something about "taking one's fun where one found it—and paying for it . . . .?"

Well—he had had his full share of fun. He had paid for it—at times in cash, at times in emotion. And now, in retrospect, he was a little ashamed.

It was queer—he reflected—how, since last night, since meeting La Sylphe, his philosophy of life, his reckoning of life's values, had changed. For, until last night, his ideal of a worth-while existence had centered about a smart Hispano-Suiza car upholstered in maroon-colored, cordovan leather, Waterloo brandy, brown sherry 1837, a stiff game of contract bridge, perfectly creased trousers, English sporting prints, and —of course—a regiment of women. And today .... Why—today he felt positively monogamous; looked with disapproval and intolerance on all men who were not; said to himself, with almost episcopal unction, in accents reminiscent of his uncle, the Bishop:

"There is something in the old-fashioned, Puritan viewpoint."

The next moment, being a sane young American and not at all hypocritical, he laughed at his own, so recently developed virtuousness and chaste, moral rectitude and drove on, down the road toward Marly-le-Roi—passing through the outskirts of town where Paris mellowed into a respectable, middle-class dotage of drab and gray and flat green, with here and there a red brick roof, like a nodding bright flower on an ancient dame's sober Sunday bonnet.

Then, presently, he reached the countryside.

The French countryside. Different from that which abutted on his native New York—from Westchester County—Long Island—New Jersey—Connecticut-not to mention billboards.

"*See America First!*" Garth remembered the patriotic slogan coined by railway people, hotel keepers, automobile manufacturers, gasolene stations, tourists' camps, and owners of hot dog and barbecue stands . . . . and he smiled as he added in his thoughts:

"See America first—provided you can find it behind the billboards!"

Billboards that were garishly painted, gorgeously illuminated, hugely lettered. Billboards that, in their own, clamorous, riotous, clowning fashion, boomed out the fantastic, incredible New World epic—while here, on the outskirts of Paris, the Old World lyric was being chanted by quaint little fields in a neat checkerboard pattern of yellow and russet and deep brown, punctured occasionally by the gables of farm houses and anæmic church spires, and a shimmer of rippling water where oak and larch and poplar dipped their dark arms to the murmur of the Seine.

Finally the roadster bumped over the lumpy cobblestones of Marly-le-Roi. It stopped before *L'Auberge des Trois Rois*, the local inn.

There the proprietor—whose severe, hieratic, rather pre-Raphaelite features gave the lie to his paunch and the lewd wink in his watery, blue eyes—recognized Garth and greeted him with pleasure.

"Welcome, M. Brent!" he cried; and, with a cough that, meant to be discreet, achieved the opposite result: "Madame—I suppose—will join you?"

"This time I am a celibate, M. Signorel. Nor is my name—this time—Brent."

"Pardon?"

"Call me Smith. Such a sound, decent, moral name

—don't you think? You see—" Garth invented rapidly, to mollify the other's curiosity, to put him on his honor, and stop all gossip that might give him away—"I am here incognito—and in danger . . . ."

"In danger . . . .?"

"Yes. A South American—a jealous husband—a violent person with a pistol—is on my track and threatening me. And so I beg you to . . . ."

"Say no more, M.—ah—Smith," M. Signorel assured him in a conspirator's whispered basso profundo. "Your secret is safely locked in my bosom. Personally, I consider jealous husbands grossly unsympathetic."

"*Vive la France!*" laughed the American; and he accompanied the other upstairs where he was shown into a comfortable suite.

A private telephone was in one of the rooms. He used it immediately—and twice.

First he called up M. Poret at the Bureau of Registry.

"Look up Courvoisier's card, M. Poret?"

"Yes."

"Any startling information?"

"Not exactly startling. But—perhaps—significant. Courvoisier seems to be a gambler; seems to have lost a lot of money on the stock exchange. And, these last few weeks, he has been a frequent visitor at the Club of the Failures. Nothing else . . . ."

"Plenty. Two and two make four . . . ."

"And, at times, five—*hein* . . . .?"

"Precisely. Thanks a lot, M. Poret."

Garth rang off; and, a few seconds later, called up his own apartment and got George on the wire. He gave him his new address; instructed him to come with the trunks as soon as possible; and asked him if anything had happened during his absence.

"Yes, Cap," replied George. "Somethin' sho'-enough *did* happen. Fo' a foreign gen'l'man came to see you—a Dook or a Count he sed he was."

"Didn't he give his name?"

"Yes, suh. Tom Ashton. Don't sound like no Dook's name to me . . . ."

"Tom Ashton? Are you positive?"

"Yes, suh."

Garth wondered who his visitor might have been. Then, suddenly, an idea came to him.

"You don't mean Tomashin by any chance?" he demanded. "Prince Tomashin?"

"Dot's wot I sed. Tom Ashton. Tall gent wid his arm in a sling. An' he an' I had a few words—an' I threw him out on his haid . . . ."

"Good Lord!"

"Yes, suh. I—" with a sort of careless pride—"I threw him out on his haid so ha'd he damn near sprained a ankle."

"Mind letting me know what you did that for?"

And George explained.

It appeared that, shortly after Garth had left his

apartment, Tomashin had called, had inquired for him, and had been told by the servant that, quite unexpectedly, his employer had decided to take this afternoon's Blue Train for Monte Carlo. Tomashin had gone. But, an hour later, he had returned. He had informed George that he had been to the railway depot; had arrived there twenty minutes before the departure of the train; had thoroughly searched platform and cars; and had found no trace of Mr. Garth Brent. The latter—he had added—was doubtless still in Paris. He had insisted on knowing where he was, saying it was a matter of vital importance; had finally tried to bribe the servant . . . .

"An' Cap," continued George, "dat dough he offered looked dog-gone good to me—an' so I took it."

"Oh—you didn't!"

"I did."

"Heavens!"

"One thousand francs—an' it's in my jeans right now—yes, suh! But—" with a sudden outburst of wild, jungly, African cachinnations—"I tells dat Dook no' mo' dan I told him befo'. I sticks like glue to my little story—dat you've done taken de Blue Train. An' den de Dook gets nasty—real nasty. Foul names he calls me—calls me a low-down heathen—an' me a good Baptist! Calls me a no-account black savage . . . . an' I sho'-enough *gits* savage—yes, suh, nuthin' but—an' I throws him out on his haid!"

Garth was disturbed as well as amused—disturbed

because his ruse had been so quickly seen through; amused at George's perfidy.

"Fine and dandy!" he congratulated him. "Just for that I present you with that braided, black jacket of mine that you've been coveting for a long time."

"Thank you, Cap."

"Anything else happen?"

"Telegram came a few minutes back."

"Open it—and read it to me."

A pause.

Then, plaintively:

"It's in French, suh."

"I don't care. High time for you to cultivate a Parisian accent. Go to it!"

George sighed—and obeyed, pronouncing the French sentences with a heavy Alabama drawl.

The telegram was signed by La Sylphe. She wired that she wanted Garth to be, around midnight, at a certain cabaret-restaurant called Le Caveau. She would come there, too, straight from the theatre. He should not speak to her, nor pay any attention to her; but should watch her closely, as he had watched her on the night before; should, later on, shadow her discreetly. For she had agreed to meet Tomashin there. The latter had sent her word that her brother Danielo wished to talk to her and that he would take her to him. But she was afraid to be alone. She needed Garth. She begged him to come and took for granted that he would—asking him not to communicate with her in the meantime; neither at her hotel, since she would be at the theatre all afternoon, rehearsing a new Indo-Chinese dance; nor at the theatre, since she would have very little time between the rehearsal and the evening performance and was badly in need of the short rest. Nor, finally, did she want him to wait for her at the stage door.

Thus the lengthy, explicit message which George transmitted painfully in his execrable French.

Garth laughed.

"Splendid, George!" he said. "Help yourself to the striped trousers too—the ones that match the braided coat—and the double-breasted, gray vest."

He clicked back the receiver. He was in a happy frame of mind; was elated at the thought that La Sylphe trusted him, that, so soon, she had taken him at his word and asked him to protect her.

He remembered the Caveau. It was a queer and unsavory place, situated in a queer and unsavory neighborhood. He wondered why Tomashin had picked it as his choice of rendezvous with La Sylphe; decided, a few moments later, that he understood the reason.

For, according to M. Poret, last night's events at the Club of Failures were known, at least unofficially, to the French government. It was conceivable—similar things had happened before, in Europe and, perhaps, in America—that, again unofficially and quite illegally, the authorities might arrest Danielo and keep him sequestered and out of the way of political mischief until after the passing of the zero hour, the date of his coming of age a week from Saturday.

Thus, most likely, the young Prince had left the club for a safer refuge. And where, in all Paris, was there a better hiding place than the ancient streets that moiled about the Caveau . . . .?

Streets so narrow that, overhead, the roofs on both sides seemed to mingle and interlace like rigging in a fishing harbor. Streets where, hardly ever, the sun penetrated. Streets plunged, at night, into bitter, blotched darkness, yet with sudden, brutish flickerings and stabbings of light that showed sights which a man would rather not see. Streets crowded with little cafés and restaurants and bistros, their fly-specked windows full of blue and green and opal rifts of smoke reminiscent of a muddy aquarium and, in back of the windows, faces bobbing whitely like shoals of evil, bloated fish. Streets where policemen were conspicuous, and therefore secure, by their absence.

Streets like a grotesque, incredible setting for a grotesque, incredible melodrama.

Streets of vice gilded and vice drab.

Streets where lips were greedy for kisses, since hands were greedy for gold.

Luxury—in these streets—and dirt. Silk and rags. Scent of musk and scent of garbage. Color of passion and color of pestilence.

A Paris symphony . . . .

Garth was familiar with the neighborhood; was familiar, too, with the Caveau itself. So he would have preferred escorting La Sylphe there.

But a moment's reflection proved to him that she was right. The two of them must not be seen together. For Tomashin—the more so since he had found out that Garth was still in Paris—would surely employ agents to watch her and to report on any stranger who might be observed in her company. On the other hand, the only time Tomashin had seen Garth had been last night, at the club, when the American had worn a face mask. Therefore the latter would pass unnoticed and unrecognized amongst the habitués and the sight-seeing tourists who usually packed the Caveau.

Besides La Sylphe would undoubtedly take one of the regular taxicabs—belonging to the *Service Supérieur*, a well-established and respectable concern—that had the parking privilege outside the theatre. So she would be safe enough until she reached the cabaret. Afterwards—thought Garth—it was up to him to watch and guard her.

He consulted his watch. It was getting on towards five.

He decided that he would while away the hours until he met La Sylphe by a cocktail or two, a decent dinner, perhaps a show.

He telephoned to Charles de Montfort at the Bureau of Registry.

"Anything on for tonight?"

"Nothing special."

"Dine with me?"

"Gladly."

"Don't dress, Charles."

"What seems to be the trouble? Put your party clothes in hock?"

"No. But I left town rather hurriedly."

"With whom? Do I know her?"

"Don't be French—and indecent!"

"And don't *you* be Anglo-Saxon—and hypocritical! After all, I remember occasions—little Suzette, for instance—not to mention others . . . ."

"Forget it! I'm a reformed character."

"Growing a halo—or is it old age creeping on? Why—consider how singularly unattractive the world would be without the flesh and the devil . . . ."

"Cut out the heavy jocosity—and meet me at the Ritz bar around six. I'll take you to Fouquet's to dine."

"Fouquet's? Where they charge fifty francs for a peach . . . .?"

"You can have seventeen peaches. Didn't I tell you that . . . .?"

"Oh yes. I remember. Something about a millionaire paying you a quite fabulous sum of money because of your beautiful eyes and your boyish smile. A female millionaire, I suppose? An elderly female millionaire with halitosis—and a wart on her left nostril—*and* the good old cosmic urge—taking a fancy to young American gigolo who . . . ."

"Oh—shut up, Charles! You give me a pain in the neck."

Garth left the inn. He drove leisurely and, shortly before six, was at the Ritz bar, waiting for his friend.

The usual crowd was there. Consciously cosmopolitan. As consciously smart. Speaking all languages and pronouncing them all, including their native tongues, with a decided accent.

A few Frenchmen. But, mostly, foreigners. All brands and degrees of foreigners.

A drove of Brazilians, wearing whatever happened to be most exclusively and expensively bad taste. British cads and American bounders, hating and ridiculing each other, but, temporarily, forgetting both hate and ridicule in their mutual dislike of the French. A German nobleman, drinking bottled Munich beer with an air of political and patriotic protest. A paunchy Chinese from the embassy in peacock-blue satin embroidered with tiny, rose-red butterflies, staring with deliberate imperturbability through his ludicrous, gold-rimmed monocle. A Kentucky colonel, speaking of the glorious days "befo' the war, suh," to a Russian Grand Duke who spoke of the glorious days "before the Bolshevist revolution—*akh—bozhe moy!*" A plum-colored cannibal princeling, loyal subject of France, sporting the crimson ribbon of the Legion of Honor on his savage breast. A Lutheran clergyman from Switzerland—and Garth wondered how *he* had got here—with dusty frock-coat, dusty side-whiskers, and dusty intolerance. An Arab aristocrat, hawkish, burnoused, contemptuous, statuesque, thinking, with morose regret, of the days of his youth in the free, yellow, brittle desert.

And, of course, the women after their kind. Women of the world and women of the half-world; the former trying to ape the latter; the latter reversing the process; and both, in consequence, succeeding as well as failing, since they looked alike, acted alike, and, doubtless, reacted alike. Many of the women seemed queerly impersonal, queerly unhuman; were like figurantes, like the painted, silent mummers of a tragi-comedy that was daily performed.

Everybody here was on the make. Everybody was endeavoring to squeeze something, in cash or sensation, from everybody else—man from woman and woman from man, man from man and woman from woman. For the Island of Cytherea was well represented. Nor was Lesbos absent.

It was typical that the flowers in the vases were quite beautiful—and quite unreal, made of silk and paper crepe. It was all in baroque contrast, with itself and with facts. It was all strident and garish and diamond-hard. It was all stucco and tinsel and spangles and bright chromium.

It crystallized, within its four walls, the Paris which France hates—as America, West of the Hudson, hates

New York's Broadway and Park Avenue. It was the only Paris which these people knew.

"Extraordinary place," said an English Duchess of recent Kansas City origin. For the last half hour she had been coining this epigram. Now she was ready to give it to the world, *her* world: "Exactly the sort of place which the lower middle-classes see nightly in their films!"

"Quite so, darling," agreed her companion, who was not the Duke—the latter being at the other end of the bar, "makin' the runnin'," as he expressed it, with the twice divorced Argentine wife of a Swedish attaché of legation.

Near by a famous Chicago newspaper correspondent, as he was meant to, had overheard the Duchess' remark. He picked it up, embroidered it, and tossed it wide.

He added:

"You know—this burg puts me in mind of my mistress. They're both so darned genuine and spontaneous—when it comes to life's two essentials—at least where the female of the species is concerned."

"You mean beauty and brain, Mac?"

"Like my foot I do, Jack! I mean immorality—and stupidity."

"Immorality is so frightfully old-fashioned," sighed a very young man whose honey-colored hair was permanently waved.

"Well—I'm an old-fashioned guy. I'm all for the pies my grandmother used to bake . . . ."

"But not for the women your grandfather used to make—eh . . . .?"

A ripple of light laughter. Others chiming in, eager for applause—until the Duchess, seeing that the exchange of wise-cracks and witticisms was getting beyond her control and therefore, vicariously, injuring her own reputation for intellectual brilliancy, decided to wind it up with a final twist of dialectic acrobatics.

She pointed through the window, at the horizon where slowly, beneath the sweep of evening, the town was changing from a purple, jagged, sardonic silhouette to an indefinite, wiped-over blur.

"Look!" she said. "Paris! Our Paris! A mixture of caviare and cabbage, platinum and pinchbeck, absinthe and holy-water, essence of rose and essence of gutter . . . . and everything for sale!"

"Including yourself, my dear old trout!" came the audible whisper of His Grace the Duke from the farther end of the bar.

There was more laughter. Garth was mildly amused, mildly bored. He grew less bored as, at his elbow, some of the men commented on the fact that, since noon, there had been on the Paris *bourse* a steady rise in the shares of munition and airplane factories—due to the situation in Wallachia where, according to the Chicago newspaper correspondent, "hell is going to bust its hinges a week from Saturday."

"Damn these rowdy little fox-terrier nations!" exclaimed a red-faced, purse-mouthed Yorkshireman.

"All they're good for is to make trouble for the rest of the world."

"Don't forget the profits," suggested the newspaperman. "Creuzot common stock went up fifteen points today—McVickar twelve—and Fokker almost twenty. Take my tip. Buy all the Creuzot you can."

"Think so?"

"Know so. I've got the inside dope. Listen, boys . . . ."

His voice dropped to a confidential drone. But Garth, sharp-eared, heard more than a little.

"This afternoon," the man from Chicago was relating, "one of the main guys in the royalist movement called on me. Bird called Tomashin. He told me, strictly on the q. t., that, a week from Saturday, Prince Danielo will enter the capital of Wallachia and claim the throne just as sure as God made little green apples. He begged me to play the game his way . . . ."

"What can *you* do, Mac?"

"The well-known power of the Fourth Estate, the press, old son!"

"Oh—making propaganda for the royalists . . . .?"

"You've said it. Tomashin offered . . . ."

"Graft?"—bluntly.

"He offered genteel but lucrative inducements, you coarse-grained, tactless Britisher! At all events, take my tip and load up on Creuzot—on all munition stocks—and you'll be in the big money, boys. We're in for another merry little, international rumpus."

And the Chicagoan fell to whistling "*Parley-voo*," and, shortly afterwards, Charles de Montfort came in and joined Garth.

"Sorry to have kept you waiting," he apologized. "Lots of work at the office. Just as I was leaving, more requests came to the Bureau . . . ."

"For the little cards?"

"Yes. By the way—" Charles lowered his voice, stared at the other—"how thick are you with Poret?"

"Fairly thick. Why?"

"Because I happened to mention to him that I was going to dine with you. And he asked me to tell you that the request for the cards came from the Foreign Ministry—and that this request was for the same cards which you studied earlier in the day."

"I see."

"Well—I don't. Mind letting me know what's between you and Poret?"

"I'd rather not."

"Oh—" Charles was a little hurt—"just as you wish. Although I can guess—something." He ordered a cocktail. "Seems the Wallachian pot is about to boil over. Seen the evening papers?"

"Not yet. What do they have to say?"

"They're absolutely hectic, panic-stricken. You see —both Italy and Germany have announced, through semi-official channels, that they'll recognize Danielo if he mounts the throne."

"While the French will keep on throwing in their influence on the side of the Wallachian republic . . . .?"

"Of course. We've got to. It's vital to us." Charles paused. He went on: "There's something else Poret asked me to tell you . . . ."

"Let's hear it."

"The French Intelligence Service has discovered a promise made by Mussolini to the royalists that, in case Danielo is crowned, Princess Maria di Savoia, the youngest daughter of the King of Italy, will become his bride. Which means that . . . ."

"Which means that if France, as she's bound to, sends a few brigades, or at least some hand-picked officers, to help the Wallachian republic, she'll be actively supporting the enemies of the King of Italy's son-in-law. And then the fat'll be on the fire—eh . . . .?"

"And how—as you Americans say!"

It was this news, these rumors, on which the Paris *bourse*, and Wall Street and the London stock exchange, had based their bull market . . . . since war spelled profit—to some.

So the Chicagoan was declaring. War—he said—was good for business, since factories, and principally American factories, would supply all combatants with the steely necessities of strife—on a strictly cash basis.

"You bet!" he announced, turning his back to the bar and facing the whole room.

His was a happy twist and quirk of phrase—chiefly when, as today, he had been mixing generous portions of champagne and stout. He described now what, doubtless at this very moment, with conflict in the air, was happening in America. He described it picturesquely, dramatically, enjoying himself thoroughly.

"Take a look across the Atlantic!" he bellowed, glass in hand. "Listen to the bully Yankee chorus! Dynamos throbbing! Bit-braces zumming and humming! Trip-hammers thudding! Derrick-cranes hoisting away! Gas-engines hissing and popping and stuttering! Piling-gins shaking and drumming! Gudgeons sliding smoothly, wickedly, into shafts! Pliers tearing and wrenching and cutting! Sure—all America getting busy—while you Europeans—you poor, lousy, unfortunate suckers—are paying us and killing each other!"

He gave a hooting laugh.

"War!" he yelled. "Three hearty cheers for war!"

War was already here, in the Ritz bar, in miniature, as people's opinions began to clash.

"Is England going to take a hand in the game?" a Spaniard asked the Yorkshireman.

"Shouldn't wonder."

"A hand—in the game?" sneered a Frenchman. "A hand—more likely—in Wallachia's pocket. England has always reminded me of a pious old, international sneak-thief dressed in black bombazine."

"And France," was the angry rejoinder, "has always reminded me of an international cocotte selling her kisses to the highest bidder."

The Lutheran clergyman considered it his duty to pour oil on troubled waters.

"Both England and France have their responsibilities," he announced in greasy pulpit tones. "France towards art—culture—*belles-lettres* . . . . while England—ah—is ever ready to take up the White Man's burden . . . ."

"Sure!" interrupted another American. "Take up the White Man's burden—and put it on the coon!"

More heated words. Spanish against Portuguese; Dutch against Belgian; German against Russian; British against French; the Chicago newspaperman sicking them on like dogs; while Garth and Charles, having finished their cocktails, went over to Fouquet's for dinner—a very excellent dinner, since the headwaiter there, like many Paris headwaiters, respected Garth Brent.

Not because of his reckless tipping. For Brazilians, too, tip handsomely. So do Argentinians, Hungarians, and Greeks. Still—is there a Paris, or even a Brussels, headwaiter who respects, really respects—any of the latter nationalities; who would not, almost by instinct, assign them to tables in draughty corners and in back of potted, dusty palms where they are unable to see or be seen?

No. Garth's popularity had nothing to do with tipping; but . . . .

Listen to him. At Fouquet's. Talking to the headwaiter who came gliding across the floor in a series of seven magnificent salaams.

"How are you, Henri?"

"Delighted to see you, M. Brent. What shall it be tonight?"

"Dry martini—very dry. Unsalted caviare—very unsalted."

"For soup—may I suggest *Paysanne?*"

"Oh—you are so hopelessly, provincially French! An American soup is indicated."

"Pardon?" Henri drew up his eyebrows. "American . . . .?"

"Precisely. I hate to hurt your patriotic feelings. But there is no soup like clam-chowder. It is the great republic's greatest culinary achievement. Some months ago, in a moment of generosity, I gave your chef the recipe. Will you ask him to . . . .?"

"Gladly, M. Brent."

"A bottle of Chambertin 1897 with the chowder."

"As to entrée . . . ."

"Entrées bore me, Henri. They are meant for chorus girls and stock brokers and similar objectionable persons. We shall proceed directly to the main course—*caneton à la presse*—a decent quart of Beaujolais to go with it. And you may choose the rest of the dinner yourself."

"Thank you, M. Brent."

And so, an hour and a half later, over a glass of superlative Waterloo brandy with its proper accessories of black coffee and aromatic Partaga cigars, the two friends were once more discussing Wallachian affairs—with Charles presently saying:

"Nine o'clock. Shall we adjourn to the Club Cosmopolite?"

"Don't feel like it. It'll mean a long bridge session—and I've got to meet somebody after a while."

"At what time?"

"Around midnight."

"Almost three hours until then. What about dropping in at a show—the Ambassadeurs for instance . . . .?"

The Ambassadeurs—thought Garth—the theatre where La Sylphe danced. Well—why not? He was not going against her wishes by watching her from the audience . . . .

"Good idea," he said.

He finished his cognac, paid, and they drove to the theatre, arriving there toward the middle of the first half of the vaudeville bill.

It was the usual, typically European vaudeville bill. Typically European in so far as most of the turns were typically American—including the trained seals that came from Alaska.

There were the two Chicago hoofers, he a thin, lithe George-Cohanesque man, she a carbon copy of the late Lillian Russell. The two Bowery-born-and-bred Chinese half-castes who did a Cantonese act in the sort of Oriental costume which is never seen East of Suez. The trick bicyclists. The "Flying McDermotts." Miss Josephine Turner, the "high-yaller" Blues singer, who—scandal spoke truth—had been kept last year by a prominent New York banker, and was being kept this year by a grandee of Spain whose haughty family traditions reached back to the days when the Abencerrage caliphs were Kings of Granada.

"Perhaps," was Garth's mocking comment, "she's the descendant of some African slave girl brought across the Straits of Gibraltar by the grandee's Arab forefather . . . ."

"Yes," agreed Charles. "And perhaps last year's New York banker is the descendant of the Jewish merchant who advanced to the grandee's ancestor the money with which to buy the slave . . . ."

Anyway, here she was, jungly, untamed, swinging her hips, chanting, in her deep-throated, quivering voice, the plaint of a whole race in darkness:

"Oh some folks claim dat de weary blues ain't bad—
Yes—some folks say dat de weary blues ain't bad—

But Ah tells you folks—
Ah tells you true—
It's de dog-gonest feelin' dat dis niggah ever had . . . ."

Thunderous applause. Then other performers. Snappy. Quick. Smart. Wise-cracking. Full of pep. The sort of vaudevillians who read *Variety* and the *Billboard* as the late William J. Bryan read the Bible; whose *One More River to Jordan* was the hope of a jump from Oshkosh to Broadway and from the four-a-day to the two-a-day; whose greatest ambition—indeed a royal accolade, a "Rise, sir knight!"—was the call to Europe, the acclaim of the Paris and London music-halls.

Singers. Dancers.

"*Somebody loves me, I wonder who . . . .*"

Shuffling feet. Tapping feet. Bright spot lights. Droning, teasing saxophones.

"*Oh mamma . . . . here we are . . . .*
Oh so far . . . . from Omaha . . . ."

Shuffle. Shuffle. Tense thighs. Bouncing, hectic feet.

In the first half of the programme only one number was not American. This number had been rapidly thought out, rehearsed, and interpolated. It was a timely number, based upon the exciting news from Wallachia, the mysterious absence of Prince Danielo, the rumor that—a week from Saturday—he would stage a melodramatic entrance into the capital of his native land. It showed Paul Fayal, the inimitable burlesque comedian, rushing out of the wings, accompanied by a bevy of half-naked chorus girls and dressed in what Paris fondly imagined was the costume of a Wallachian aristocrat: a farcical mingling of bushy whiskers, sable furs, knee-high, red boots, curved scimitars, vodka bottles, and a knout made of papier-maché.

Peering right and left with all the time-hallowed gags of a stage conspirator, he introduced himself to the audience with a cavernous, sibilant:

"Sh-sh-sh! I am Prince Danielo, the great Wallachian enigma!"

Then he executed an eccentric dance which was one third Cossack, one third cake-walk, and one third Hungarian czardas, and sang a song with the refrain:

"Boum! Boum! Boum!
En avant la révolution!"

He followed it by another dance in which the chorus girls joined. He whipped their calves with his papier-maché knout. And he was off to the pizzicato of a dozen guitars and mandolins that were striving desperately to syncopate the Wallachian national anthem.

More applause.

The first half of the programme was over.

The men left their seats. Some to go to the bar on the upper balcony. Others—not Parisians they, but provincial Frenchmen and foreigners, here without their wives, thus relaxed into careless joviality—to stroll up and down the promenoir and ogle the cocottes and start the preliminaries for biological experiments . . . . like a tunnel, this promenoir, a tunnel of shameless, naked flesh, made light and brilliant by gay gowns, rouge, jewels . . . .

Then there were loud words:

"*Messieurs et Mesdames* . . . ."

The people stopped. They turned and looked toward the stage.

A splendidly bearded gentleman in full evening dress, the manager of the Ambassadeurs, had stepped before the curtains. He expressed his regret—ah—his desolation and despair because—alas!—so unfortunately—La Sylphe would be unable to give her performance tonight . . . .

Garth heard. He was startled.

He remembered the telegram which she had sent him, telling him that she would rehearse all afternoon—would rest until the evening show . . . .

What could have happened . . . .?

Had she, perhaps, been taken ill . . . .?

He was terribly disturbed. He jumped up. He left, with a muttered word of apology to Charles. He hurried to the stage door.

There Doderet, the uniformed door man, was on guard. He shook his head when Garth demanded information about La Sylphe.

"Against the house rules."

"Here—" the American gave him money—"to counteract the house rules. Is La Sylphe ill?"

"No."

"But—where is she . . . .?"

"She has gone away. Out of town."

"Eh . . . .? Out of town . . . .?"

"Indeed."

"Impossible!"

"I assure you it is so." Doderet swelled with self-importance. "I, personally, telephoned to the railway station and made the reservation for her."

"But—why . . . .?"

"Doubtless because of the telegram—the news she must have received—she seemed upset . . . ."

"I see. And the reservation you made—tell me—where to . . . .?"

"To Lyons."

Lyons—thought Garth—the town where her older brother, Karolus, was in the Hospital of the Ursuline Sisters. And the telegram . . . .? Perhaps Karolus' condition was dangerous—she had hastened to his bedside . . . .? Yes—that must be it . . . .

Then a suspicion came to him.

"Look here," he asked. "Any idea what time the telegram arrived?"

"Around two o'clock."

"Sure of it?"

"Absolutely sure. Her train for Lyons left at three. She had me call a taxicab for her." A smile curled his gross features. Scandal—he reflected—between La Sylphe and this young foreigner. "If Monsieur wishes to know anything else . . . .?"

"No. Thank you."

"Thank *you*," said Doderet, as his rapacious hand closed around another gold piece.

He shut the door, while the American stood there, in the narrow alley cluttered with dusty stage props that led to the entrance. He frowned. He was puzzled. He told himself that her train had left at three, that she had received the telegram at two, and that she had sent *him* a wire, asking him to meet her at the Caveau, shortly after four, at the time when she was on her way to Lyons.

Therefore—he concluded—there was a slip somewhere; and his next thought was:

"O. K. about the telegram to her. Doubtless it summoned her to Lyons. But what about her message to me . . . .? A fake—sure enough. Somebody else must have sent it, signing her name, so as to get me to the Caveau, to get me—yes—into a trap. Who . . . .? Why—Tomashin—of course . . . ."

He looked up, as, a moment later, he heard Charles de Montfort's voice:

"I've been searching for you all over the place."

"I've been out here—smoking . . . ."

"That the reason you jumped up so suddenly when the manager made his announcement about La Sylphe . . . .?"

"Oh . . . ."

"What's the trouble, Garth? You seem worried."

"I *am* worried."

"Anything I can do . . . .?"

"No, no."

"Tell me just the same."

Garth shook his head. He remembered his promise to Sir Pascal.

"Can't tell you, old man," he replied. "I gave my word of honor . . . ."

"There are certain moments in life," interrupted the other, "when a word of honor can be broken—when it must be broken—when, not to break it, would mean *dis*honor. Ah—" with a Frenchman's typical, almost feminine intuition—"for instance to help a woman—whom one loves greatly."

"A woman," whispered Garth, "whom I love very, very greatly."

"As I love *you* very greatly," said Charles, again the typical Frenchman who considers emotional cold-bloodedness and self-restraint, even between man and man, a silly, rather puerile Anglo-Saxon affectation.

"I am your friend—your best friend—am I not . . . .?"

"You bet you are!"

"Then tell me . . . ."

Garth hesitated; finally made up his mind.

"All right. Let's go some place where we can have a quiet talk."

Charles pointed across the street.

"What about that bistro over there? It'll be empty this time of night."

"Come on."

They went to the bistro. It was a neat little place. Neat the zinc-lined bar. Neat the generous array of bottles. Neat the few plain pine tables and chairs. Neat the excessively yellow-haired Burgundian proprietress, built on the lines of a Percheron stallion. Neat even the flat porcelain spittoons filled with sand.

There, over a glass of rather decent Swiss beer, Garth confided to his friend everything that had occurred to him in the last twenty-four hours.

Charles smiled.

"Extraordinary!" he commented. "Charmingly unlikely and illogical! Quite the sort of picaresque adventure that would happen to a romantic, quixotic young man like you!"

"Look here—" Garth flared up a little—"I'm telling you the truth . . . ."

"The whole truth—and nothing but the truth. Of

course you are. That's just what makes it so amusing. Always getting into fantastic messes . . . ."

"And always getting out of them."

"By the skin of your teeth, as often as not. But—mark my words—some day you won't. Some day you'll be—oh—cold-shouldered by fate."

"Well—" demanded Garth—"what of it? Why—" with that sudden, amazingly un-American trick of stilted, baroque speech which was his in certain moments of elation—"I'll make shift of fate's cold shoulder—till I meet her again. And then she'll give me a warm shoulder and—by God!—a kiss or two into the bargain . . . ."

"And suppose she refuses . . . .?"

"If she refuses, it'll be my ten fingers around her throat until she squeals for mercy." He banged the table with his clenched fist. He demanded challengingly: "Or has age come upon me so quickly that I should put my stomach against the counter and earn my living selling sugar and coffee and dried codfish—and no finer excitement than a half bottle of cheap, red wine, a five franc seat in a music-hall, and, maybe, a ten franc cocotte every other Saturday night . . . .?"

Charles applauded.

"Splendid ebullition!" he exclaimed. "Grand and glorious effervescence! Our romantic young man in his most irrepressibly dithyrambic mood! Using hexameter and antistrophe to climb the heights of Parnassus!"

He laughed. Then he grew serious.

"Let's forget the purple poetry," he went on, "and return to calm, disagreeable prose. There are a few points in your story that bother me."

"For instance?"

"How did Sir Pascal acquire his gigantic fortune?"

"Damned if I know. Nor do I care so very much. What else?"

"Why, aware that Karolus had had an accident and would be unable to meet her at the Club of the Failures, did La Sylphe insist on going there?"

"The same question puzzled me for quite a while. I looked for all sorts of mysterious reasons—until I found the real one—and it's very simple . . . ."

"Namely . . . .?"

"Woman."

"Woman . . . .?"

"Woman's stubborn pride. Karolus had been injured. Very well. She was going to pull this thing off by herself—would go to the club alone, find Danielo, talk to him, persuade him. Then she recognized Tomashin—who knew her, spoke to her. And she became frightened, nervous . . . . and then she saw me—saw the decoration on my chest . . . ."

"And concluded that you were there on Sir Pascal's behest?"

"That's it."

"But why, instead of sending you, didn't he send word to her, asking her not to go to the club?"

"I guess he did. But she refused to obey. That same pride of hers—don't you see? A stubborn, self-hurting pride that seems to run in her family. Do you recall the telegram which Sir Pascal, last night, received at the Cosmopolite—and which startled him so . . . .?"

"I didn't notice at the time."

"I did. I've an idea the telegram contained La Sylphe's refusal to heed his warning. He didn't know what to do. He couldn't go himself. He's old —physically weak—useless. So he paid me to be his agent . . . ."

"Maybe you're right," replied the Frenchman. "Remains one question—or, rather, two. How did Tomashin discover Sir Pascal's, Karolus', and La Sylphe's plans? And how did he find out her double secret—the secret of her identity, and the secret that she is the guardian of the ancient, iron crown?"

"I'll tell you. Remember the interviews I had today—with Sir Pascal . . . .?"

"And Signora Cuneo?"

"Not to forget Dennis Courvoisier. These interviews confirmed what I had already surmised. Take Courvoisier first. He advised me to leave well enough alone, to cease interfering in the affairs of Wallachia. Now—he has always disliked me. Therefore, the advice was not given in a friendly spirit, but because he has something to hide. And I know what this something is. You see—he has lost money on the stock exchange—has been a frequent visitor of late at the Club of the Failures . . . ."

"And has been bribed by Tomashin to spy . . . .?"

"By Tomashin and—Signora Cuneo."

"But—she loves Sir Pascal . . . ."

"She also loves her son—and hates the former dynasty. With Courvoisier as her intermediary, she kept her son informed of all that happened."

"How did she know?"

"Sir Pascal told her. He did not suspect until to-day that her love for her son and her hate for the former dynasty is as strong—perhaps stronger—than her devotion to him. It was this truth—remember my telling you?—of which he said he was afraid, which he did not wish to know. I—oh—I shall never forget his words . . . ."

He repeated them:

" 'Often truth is an invention and snare of the Devil—an evil and accursed thing—a thing made of black magic—as poisonous as a hundred snakes—and roaring like the Apocalypse . . . .' "

He sighed. He went on to speak about these two: the man and the woman, Sir Pascal Nahadin and Carlotta Cuneo. The man who, long incarcerated in a monastery, had forgotten, within its calm, chilly, grey walls, the ambitions and turmoil and rebellion and unhappiness of the past; who had dreamt there a dream of peace—a dream of great, strong Christendom—a dream of republican freedom where there would be content and plenty and the pleasant laughter of all lowly things rising like incense to the nostrils of the Lord. The woman who, too, remembered the unhappiness and red injustice of the past, but who measured it only with the yardstick of her own passion—passion of love and passion of hate; who, because of it, would plunge Wallachia into war, would plunge the whole world into war—for the sake of personal revenge, the sake of the blind, cruel gods of Babylon whose tongues made mock of right.

And again Garth described the scene in the financier's office. He described the other scene, when he had confronted the Italian woman; while Charles, as he listened, felt the prick and tingle of one of those ironic tragedies that have been between lovers since the beginning of creation, and saw—as the American pictured them—the white, haughty face of Sir Pascal and the white, ravaged face of Signora Cuneo . . . . like dusty old portraits in a dark house, the simile came to him.

Garth was silent. The other asked:

"What's the answer to it all? What are you going to do?"

Then, when his friend did not reply immediately, he continued:

"I know what I'd do in your place."

"Well . . . .?"

"A question first. You love her . . . .?"

"But—" impatient, a little embarrassed—"I told you . . . ."

"I know you did. Only—I mean—it isn't as it was with Suzette—to pick one at random . . . .? You were nuts about her, too . . . ."

"This—this is different. If you could see her—so fine—so courageous—so simple and yet so intense—and so beautiful. Yes—risking your irreverent laughter—beautiful and shining as the sun . . . ."

"Enough said," interrupted the other. "Sounds like the genuine thing. We'll have, hereafter, the melancholy spectacle of a romantic young man who has had his wings clipped, who has reformed." He smiled. "Tell me something else. Does the female paragon return your love?"

"Oh . . . ."

"Witness, being a decent and fairly modest sort, refuses to answer—although he has his suspicions. All right then. Here's my practical advice. Go to the girl. Ask her to marry you—to become Mrs. Garth Brent—to forget all these Wallachian intrigues—and to wave, hereafter, the Stars and Stripes."

Garth was amused. But he shook his head.

"Sounds reasonable," he admitted. "Only—I can't ask her that."

"Why not? You don't care a damn about Wallachia . . . ."

"But she does, don't you see? And I love her, as I

had occasion to point out to you. And whatever is vital to her is vital to me."

"Spoken like an officer and a gentleman. Spoken like a member of that fantastic American race which puts woman on a pedestal and honors her with three daily kowtows. Therefore I repeat: what are you going to do?"

Garth consulted his watch.

"I'll stick around here for about an hour," he said. "I'll have another spot or two of beer. I've tasted much worse. Then it'll be time to drift over to the Caveau."

"The Caveau . . . .? Did I hear right . . . .?"

"Yes."

"You mean to say that you'll walk into this trap—with your eyes wide open?"

"Again—yes."

"But . . . ."

"Experience during the war," came the smiling rejoinder, "when I was busy catching the wily Heinie at his naughty little tricks, taught me that the only way to walk into a trap is—precisely—with your eyes wide open."

"I fail to understand . . . ."

"Don't be so dense! Eyes wide open to see how the trap works—and who springs it."

"Why—Prince Tomashin. Who else? You said so yourself."

"Nor have I altered my opinion. But—what, exactly, does he intend doing?"

"He intends killing you."

"Rot!"

"He tried to—last night—when he . . . ."

"When he mistook me for Karolus and when, in his benighted, South-Eastern European fashion, he considered assassination a sound and incontrovertible, political argument. Today it's different. Today he's aware of my identity. And—to kill me—as *me?* Wouldn't be worth the risk. Besides—don't forget—he doesn't know me by sight."

"He'll find out all right. The man is shrewd—and vindictive. And—the moment he realizes that you've fooled him, that you've fooled him again—there is going to be danger."

"Not very much danger—not even if he should get wise to the fact that the gaping, ingenuous tourist amongst the other gaping, ingenuous tourists at the Caveau is one Mr. Garth Brent. All he wants to do—I've an idea—is to get me out of the way temporarily. To kidnap me—in other words—and, perhaps, to try a sort of third degree on me so as to unearth how I come into the Wallachian picture."

"Dangerous just the same. Look here—I'll be a handy man to have in the background. I'll go with you."

"Glad to have you—and grateful."

"That's settled."

Charles paused. Then, suddenly, he laughed.

"What's the joke?" asked the other.

"Something that occurred to me. Listen . . . ." And when, right then, the proprietress of the bistro stepped up closely, mopping a table next to theirs, the Frenchman lowered his voice to a whisper, winding up: "What do you think?"

"Fine and dandy. But I don't see how we'll be able to get away with it. Tomashin won't be alone."

"There'll be no trouble if I can locate one man—the very man who'll help us."

"Who may he be?"

"Bibi le Farceur!"

And the Frenchman, partly in mock and partly in real admiration, almost in awe, pronounced the name with pompous solemnity, as he might say: a Bourbon, a Roosevelt, a Romanoff, or a Hohenzollern . . . .

CHAPTER TEN

GARTH, too, was thrilled.

"Bibi le Farceur!" he echoed.

For all Paris knew the fame of this Bibi le Farceur, or Bibi the Josher, as all Chicago—not to mention New York and Oshkosh and Huckleberry Corners, Mass.—knows the reputation of Scar-Face Al Capone, and as the lawless old West had known the hard, red Saga of Billy the Kid. Paris knew, by the same token, that Bibi was the undisputed chieftain of all the Apaches who "bleed the citizens" between the rue Taille-Pain and the Tour Saint-Jacques.

There, on his native heath, he ruled like a feudal German baron of a forgotten century. There, with democratic impartiality, he took toll from rich and poor alike and collected tribute from a dozen rackets. There his word was law; was even beyond the law.

Being a local political power of sorts—and again we might draw a parallel with New York and Huckleberry Corners, Mass.—he remained miraculously unjailed and undisturbed by the police. In fact, a month earlier—to the rather hypocritical wrath of the opposition press—he had come off scot-free when a wealthy stock-broker had been found robbed and badly injured in a dark, smelly alley not far from the rue Verderet, and when, after the discovery of a dagger, bearing Bibi's initials and stuck neatly between the victim's third and fourth rib, the Apache had explained that he had loaned it to a casual acquaintance whose name he was unable to recall and who had needed it to cut off the rind of a particularly tough wedge of Port-du-Salut cheese.

Therefore a valuable ally, this Bibi le Farceur; and a dangerous enemy . . . .

"How did you get to know him?" inquired Garth.

"He was in my regiment during the war. He's under a certain obligation to me—swore there's nothing he wouldn't do for me."

"Saved his life, I guess?"

"Well—indirectly. I found him asleep on sentry duty, at Verdun, and didn't report him. His natural habitat is the quarter near the Caveau." Charles rose. "I'll try and get hold of him."

"I'll come with you."

"Better not. I may have to search for him in one or two dumps. And you have all the earmarks of a young American millionaire. Would be tempting Providence. May I borrow your car?"

"Help yourself."

"I'll be back as soon as I can—within the half hour, I should imagine—whether I find him or not. Wait here for me—will you?"

"Not here. Meet me at the Claridge. I've a 'phone call to make." He shook his head, as Charles pointed at the instrument on the bar. "Long distance," he explained.

The other laughed.

"Lyons?" he demanded. "To see if you can locate the fair lady?"

"You've said it."

"What a cowardly trick!"

"Cowardly?"

"To pop the question over the telephone."

"I've no such intention."

"Only want to hear her dulcet tones, I suppose?"

"Partly," smiled the American. "But my real reason is that I'm going to tell her what has happened—about the fake telegram—and about our plan . . . ."

"To show her what a hero you are . . . .?"

"No. But when she learns that, with or without her consent, I propose barging into the Wallachian mess, well—she may change her mind—may welcome my help—and may have a valuable suggestion or two."

"Not a bad idea," agreed Charles.

He left, while Garth hurried over to Claridge's Hotel, a few blocks away.

There he consulted the railway folders. La Sylphe's train—he discovered—had reached Lyons about half an hour earlier. She was, doubtless, still at her brother's bedside. He put through a long distance call to the Hospital of the Ursuline Sisters. The trunk-line was not busy this time of the evening; and so, not many minutes later, he heard the sleepy, querulous voice of the night orderly inquiring what he desired.

"I'd like to speak to Prince Karolus."

"Wait—I'll inform the supervising nurse."

Shortly afterwards, Garth was listening to the latter's cool, efficient accents:

"Quite impossible."

"But . . . ."

"The Prince is asleep," she explained. "He has been severely injured . . . ."

"I know, I know . . . ."

"Well . . . .?"

"I didn't really want to talk to him. I want to talk to his sister . . . ."

"His—sister . . . .?"

"Yes."

"I know nothing about his sister. At least—she is not here."

"But—" Garth was startled—"she must be!"

"I assure you . . . ."

"She must be! Look here—" feverishly—"Prince Karolus sent her a telegram—begging her to come to Lyons at once . . . ."

"The Prince sent no telegram! And—" picturing to herself a drunken Parisian, intent on tactless, practical joking—"I wish you a very good evening!"

Sharply, with a little dry, dramatic click of finality, the bang of the receiver echoed in Garth's ear—echoed in his brain, his heart. He stood there. He was amazed. He was frightened.

Then, quickly, he turned back to the instrument and asked Central for the Excelsior where La Sylphe lived.

There the switchboard operator told him that La Sylphe never received telephone calls. The instructions on that point were strict.

Make an exception . . . .? No, no. Why—it was worth her job . . . .

"But—please—" he insisted—"it is a matter of life and death . . . ."

Something in Garth's voice—a note of agony, of tense, driving sincerity—convinced the girl that he was speaking the truth; persuaded her to break the rule for once.

"Wait—" she said—"I'll see . . . ."

There was a pause. He heard the buzzing of the bell in La Sylphe's apartment; heard, a minute later, the operator's words:

"Mademoiselle is not in her rooms."

"Thank you," he murmured.

"I—" with genuine sympathy—"I'm so sorry, Monsieur!"

Again the click of the receiver echoed in Garth's ear—echoed in his brain, his heart. Again he stood there, amazed, frightened; terribly frightened.

The explanation . . . .?

Simple enough.

As a faked message had reached him, in La Sylphe's name, so, surely, a faked message had reached her. She had walked into a trap—beyond the shadow of a doubt.

Oh yes—it was easy to be wise after the event.

But—where had she been called . . . .? How, in all Paris, could he find her . . . .?

"What am I going to do . . . .?" he mumbled. "Dear Lord God—what am I going to do . . . .?"

He rushed over to the Ambassadeurs, on the Champs-Elysées.

The Ambassadeurs was closing. So were the other theatres in the neighborhood: the Fémina, the Comédie, the Marigny, and the Cinéma-Colisée. Escape-seeking, pleasure-seeking men and women were debouching, a little dazed, a little beglamored, out of the swinging lobby doors. They were still half wrapped in the enchantment of the make-believe world of which, for a few short hours, they had been a coughing, feet-shuffling, yet listening and integral part. They were still keyed up to a nervous, sensuous pitch, unwilling to return to their homes and the prosy, virtuous drabness of their homes; still, most of them, questing for excitement and thrills. The pavement was brimmed with motor traffic; with rows of automobiles, glistening, honking, caught between block and block, twenty deep and eight abreast, waiting for the policeman's shrill whistle, then leaping forward like animals, mudguard scraping against mudguard, engines hot-purring, exhausts reeking, gears screeching triumphantly into first.

And so Garth had his work cut out—dodging perilously in and out between the cars; advancing against the human tide that was slow moving of necessity; pushing and elbowing his way to the stage door.

There Doderet, the door man, was talking to some chorus girls. He recognized the American, the distributor of golden largess, with reminiscent as well as anticipatory pleasure. Nor was he destined to be disappointed.

For money clinked. A question, thus paid for cash down, was asked:

"About La Sylphe—you said she went to Lyons?"

"I, personally, made the reservation for her."

"And called the taxicab, didn't you?"

"Yes."

"Remember the number . . . .?"

"But—impossible . . . ."

"Well—what sort of taxicab . . . .? Belonging to the *Service Supérieur*—or the *Compagnie Générale . . . .?*"

"Ah—Monsieur . . . ." fat shoulders shrugged; hairy hands gesticulated—"how can I remember . . . .?"

"Where did you get it?"

"It was waiting at the corner—over there—as I accompanied Mademoiselle La Sylphe to the street.

The chauffeur saw us—drove up . . . . that is all . . . ."

"Thank you."

"Thank *you*, Monsieur!"

And Doderet, when Garth had walked away, winked a bleary, disreputable eye at one of the chorus girls and whispered to her:

"Listen, little cream-puff! Romance is in the air. I, too, being a full-blooded, tender-hearted Gasçon, believe in romance . . . ."

He embraced her. He pressed his lips to hers. And she, promptly and vigorously, slapped his face.

"Take my advice, obese and impertinent hyena," she cried, "and kiss whom you please! But—" and again her hand found his cheek—"be sure that you please whom you kiss!"

Then there was laughter; laughter that, mockingly, hurtingly, jingled and reverberated in Garth's ears, as he turned down the narrow alley toward the Champs-Elysées and went back to the Claridge.

Kidnapped—he told himself—La Sylphe kidnapped —there was no doubt of it . . . .

The thought, the bitter imagining, set every nerve in him a-quiver to its utmost capacity. It filled him with black, bleak horror and fear. Horror and fear—and hate. Hate against Tomashin. Hate against Wallachia. Hate—yes—against all Europe. Europe—with its coiling, never-ceasing intrigues. Europe—ridden by the devil of pride and greed—sacrificing its finest and best for the sake of dead, stinking historical traditions—and because of them, making harlots of its women and cheap hucksters of its men . . . .

He sank down into a chair.

"What am I going to do . . . .? Dear Lord God —what am I going to do . . . .?"

He buried his head in his hands; and people passed —tourists, foreigners, who lived at the Claridge—and they looked at him and drew conclusions in keeping with their moral and ethical standards and expressed these conclusions more or less audibly.

"Drunk!" sniffed a thin-lipped, flat-chested Brooklyn Y.W.C.A. secretary, pointing at him with a bony, big-knuckled, contemptuous, self-righteous finger, acid disapproval oozing out of her rather large pores.

"Drunk!" smiled a tolerant Virginian gentleman, willing to live and let live.

"Drunk!" commented a hearty, leather-skinned Alaskan sour-dough, come to Europe to spend his pile and spoil his digestion. "Drunk—by all that's unholy!" he repeated with faint envy, because, all evening, he had been trying to do likewise and had not succeeded.

So Charles de Montfort found his friend.

He was a jubilant Charles who cried: "Listen! I got hold of Bibi—and he's willing and eager to help!"; and who became less jubilant when he saw the other's drawn, haggard features; who demanded anxiously:

"What's the matter, old man?"

Dully, hopelessly, Garth explained; and the Frenchman exclaimed how sorry he was, how terribly sorry; and then he suggested:

"Come on. Let's go."

"Where?"

"We'll search for her."

"Tonight . . . .? In Paris . . . .? Useless. Like hunting for a needle in a haystack."

"Maybe so. Still—you can't just sit here and count your toes and wait for things to happen. You've got to do—something."

"Yes, yes. Of course. Something. But—what does it mean—something . . . .? Why—" with a sort of angry, impatient dejection—"it really doesn't mean a damned thing—does it? Just a lousy bromide . . . ."

For a while neither one spoke. They were both unhappy, despondent. Presently, because the silence was getting on his nerves, Charles said:

"By the way—Bibi laughed his fool head off when I told him."

The American was vaguely interested.

"How much did you tell him?" he asked.

"Everything—except the political part. For the latter I substituted woman—the eternal triangle—jealousy—passion—murderous jealousy and passion—

the very motives which Bibi would understand and sympathize with. And he did sympathize. And—I repeat—he roared with laughter."

"Doesn't sound like sympathy to me."

"Wait till you hear the rest. Remember what you guessed—about Tomashin preparing some kind of trap for you—at the Caveau . . . .?"

"Well . . . .?"

"Bibi le Farceur is this trap," announced Charles dramatically.

"Eh . . . .?"

"He is—at least—the steely teeth in this trap. You see—funny coincidence, isn't it?—Voivenel, the owner of the Caveau, happens to be one of Bibi's henchmen. This afternoon he brought Tomashin round to Bibi's place. And Tomashin hired our Apache friend to '*tourner un truc*,' as Bibi expressed it. To pull off a dirty trick, in other words. Two dirty tricks—in fact."

"Two?"

"Yes."

"The first I know. To knock me over the head. Something of that sort. But what's the second?"

"Bibi refused to tell me. He said—with that same hooting laughter—that it didn't affect you."

"Incidentally," asked Garth, "how does Bibi expect to recognize me?"

"Tomashin—Bibi said—was going to point you out

to him. It seems he has a description of your noble Roman features."

"Thanks to Malik—I imagine—and my garrulous old janitress."

Once more Garth was silent. Once more he sat there, slumped into the chair, his head bent, his eyes gazing at the floor.

Then, suddenly, he looked up. He spoke with suppressed excitement:

"Charles, I've got it!"

"Got what?"

"The solution. The way to find La Sylphe. To free her. Not only that—" with rising enthusiasm. "Also the way to help her and Sir Pascal where Wallachia is concerned. To defeat Danielo and the royalists. Ah—" with that picaresque, romantic quirk of phrase which was his in moments of high elation—"to defeat the blind beasts of Babylon—the beasts of strife . . . ."

The Frenchman smiled. Without a doubt—he thought—Garth was himself again.

"Mussolini, I salute you!" he interrupted, raising his right hand in the Fascist manner. "And how do you expect to accomplish all these miracles?"

"Very simply. We'll carry on with our original plan."

"You mean—about the Caveau—and Tomashin . . . .?"

"Not to forget the gentle little Bibi."

"What good will that do?"

"Listen!" Garth explained rapidly and at length. He added:

"Get the idea?"

"Absolutely!"

"All right. Let's get a move on. We haven't much time to lose."

Garth jumped up. Gone was his despondency, his supine torpidity, his fear, his irresolution. Now he was ready to act with all the force of his being—a force made stronger by love and, too, by hate.

They left the Claridge. They drove, at racing speed, through the night.

It was a little after midnight that they turned into the rue des Innocents which, in memory of the daily street market, was still littered with cabbage leaves and orange peels and crushed snail shells, still pungent with the odors of countless rounds of cheese stored in the adjoining sheds. They stopped in front of No. 5. An evil, rickety, tubercular house. A signboard was moving lazily in the wind. *Au Caveau* was painted on it in Gothic letters.

They pushed open the age-gangrened door and stepped into a narrow entrance hall which was almost completely filled by an enormous zinc-and-wood counter presided over by a green-aproned barman.

He gave them the customary salutation of the place:

"*Bon soir, sout-neurs*—good evening, pimps!" he yelled.

"*Et ta mère, maquereau*—and what about your mother?" Charles acknowledged the greeting in a similarly ribald manner.

Then he asked for Voivenel, the proprietor, who came a moment later.

He was lean and angular. The nose, the ears, the uptilted chin that rose defiantly to meet the sardonic lower lip, the eyebrows, the thin, long, flexible mouth, the curve of the slim hips, the very feet in their padded felt slippers—everything was in sharp angles. Sharply, angular, too, were his words in which he assured them that the whole matter had been properly arranged, asked them to follow him, and took them down a dark stairway into a little room from which, through the cleft of the half open door, they had a good view of the Caveau itself.

A queer place—the Caveau.

Until the French revolution it had been an underground monastery occupied by monks—the simple, illiterate, pious peasant-monks of Brabant and Picardy. Then, when the impatient democracy of France had brushed away the cobwebs of Bourbon and Rome with an iron fist, an enterprising Burgundian wine merchant—great-grandfather of the reigning Voivenel—had purchased the premises, had turned the low, vaulted cells into boxes and drinking dens, and had commenced to collect toll from the less reputable elements of society.

So no longer—and according to your political and

religious convictions you will deem it progress or retrogression—the place echoed the tinkling of tiny prayer bells, the solemn, sonorous chanting of "Hail Mary" and "*Mater Dolorosa.*" Instead—the melancholy, rather nauseating thought came to Garth—it echoed the clinking of glasses, the belching of alcoholic voices, the shrieking of lewd songs and lewder jokes.

The pathetic little, crude paintings of the Virgin and the Child that had once adorned the damp, lichened walls and made them holy, had been plastered over and were scrawled with puerile, indecent drawings and bits of obscene prose and verse and the signatures of thief and burglar and assassin, of Apache and anarchist. The monks themselves were dead and buried and their places taken by the jetsam and flotsam of humanity . . . . sodden, wicked, crushed by their own gross, fleshly desires; with the heat and stench of the thieves' kitchen about them and the cloying reek of strange, pagan vices; leaning across table-tops slopped and cluttered with fouled plates and sticky bottles and glasses; talking in raucous, metallic, staccato slang to the painted women by their sides; their fingers pawing, with the same pleasure, breasts flaccid and breasts rigid; their coarse faces a silently villainous recounting of most villainous deeds; their loose lips swapping blasphemous, sadistic tales which discredited the narrator almost equally whether they were true or not—and, here and there, a gaping, nervous tourist, out for a second-hand thrill . . . .

Watching the scene from the small room were Charles and Garth. They had sat down not far from the half open door, in a shadowy corner where they could see without being seen.

The American was silent. He was in a peculiar state of mind.

He went over the happenings of the past hours. A little more than twenty-four hours. A night—and a day—and another night.

Such a short space of time.

And yet, within its narrow limits, he had—it seemed to him—lived through as many lives as a cat. Within its narrow limits, he had beheld, and played a part in, drama, melodrama, tragedy, and ludicrous comedy. He had lost his money—had regained comparative affluence, thanks to a fantastic multimillionaire sending him on a fantastic errand—had acted, involuntarily, a mysterious rôle in a mysterious political intrigue—had fought a duel—had escaped death by the thinnest of thin margins—had fallen in love, gloriously, overwhelmingly, with a masked dancer who had turned out to be a Princess of the blood.

Thus fate had clashed and thundered unthinkable, incredible, fabulous, and rather garish wings about his amazed ears. Chance, the blind Madonna, had taken a hand in the game. He had cocked a tattered, arrogant feather at drab, prosy, every-day life—and had encountered romance—living romance, romance in the flesh.

And why not?—he asked himself; replied to himself that, at times, romance had a disconcerting trick of being true; so much more true than mere realism.

Oh yes—thought this romantic young man, a queer, high triumph singing in his heart—there were things in this world besides sullen engines and sulky mathematics and cold, efficient machines. There was still—surely would ever be—love and hate, white love and hate as red as wine, as red as death.

A man—considered Garth, smiling at his own imagining—might drive an automobile or pilot an airplane, yet might be wearing golden spurs upon his heels and a crested helmet upon his head . . . .

He interrupted his thoughts as a shifting of the crowd in the Caveau brought a table, quite near the stairway, into the focus.

He pointed.

"Look," he whispered to his friend. "See that short, swarthy man over there? That's Malik—the bird who tried to shoot me. And the other is Tomashin—I know him by the scar on his jaw . . . ."

The two sat facing the entrance. They seemed expectant, waiting.

"Waiting for us," said Charles.

"And for Bibi."

"We've a surprise in store—eh?"

"You bet!"

Presently the outer door opened. Some people entered. And this time it was Charles who explained:

"Bibi le Farceur and his gang."

"Bibi le Farceur and his gang!" an admiring chorus ran round the Caveau's dirty, scrawled walls.

There were half a dozen of them. They crowded about a table.

Five were men. One was a girl.

The five men were very much alike as to shrewd, vulpine, clean-shaven features, peaked tweed caps jauntily pushed back on bullet-shaped, closely cropped skulls, peg-top trousers of black velveteen tightly encircling the ankles, fringed, crimson sashes drawn about waspish waists, a final touch of effeminacy given by the yellow, pointed, buttoned, meticulously polished shoes. Nor did Bibi himself differ much from his henchmen; could only be picked out by the feudal deference with which the other gangsters treated him.

They seemed—reflected Garth—almost too genuine. They seemed almost theatrical—and perhaps enjoying this very theatricality—in being, precisely, the typical Apaches as Paris imagines them.

The girl with them was dressed with cheap, glaring ornateness. But she was startlingly beautiful; with a thick mane of auburn hair, a short, high-bridged nose, a scarlet, sensuous gash of a mouth, and great eyes as green as a cat's.

Garth looked at her. He was attracted, interested.

"A woman," he commented, the Old Adam in him peeping out a little, "to be loved greatly." Hurriedly he added: "I mean—of course—were I not in love with somebody else."

The Frenchman laughed.

"A woman," he replied, "to be avoided greatly. For she is Casque d'Or. She belongs to Bibi. And local rumor has it that he's knifed several reckless young gentlemen who looked too deeply into her eyes . . . ."

So the two friends conversed. They conversed—if the truth be told—less profoundly than vividly about this and that and the other thing; and they sipped their exceedingly bad wine with a sort of astonished distaste; and watched Tomashin and Malik—who, in their turn, were anxiously watching the outer door.

"Watching for you," Charles told the other. "The cat watching for the mouse . . . ."

"A mouse with teeth and claws."

Then, when the great bronze bell in the nearby Church of Saint-Roch boomed out the muffled sob of the half hour, the Frenchman said:

"Your signal, old man. Hop along."

The American left the back room. He climbed the dark stairway, crossed the bar, and, using the other stairway, entered the Caveau properly speaking where he was piloted to a table, midway between Tomashin's and Bibi's, by the bull-throated, bare-armed ex-burglar who was head-waiter and who had been tipped off by Voivenel. And so the various members of the drama were assembled—a drama that, shortly afterwards, peaked to a lurid climax, although not according to the way Tomashin had rehearsed it.

Nothing wrong with the manner in which he played his own part. He sought the Apache's eye. He raised his wine glass. He gestured with it towards the American, as if to say:

"This is he. Do your stuff, Bibi!"

The latter rose with a curse. At once a grimly expectant hush fell over the Caveau. The music—a drunken Maltese sailor was twanging a guitar—broke off with a jarring discord. A waiter dropped a bottle. People shifted in their seats, stared, trembled a little. For Bibi le Farceur was Bibi le Farceur.

Tomashin smiled; stopped smiling as the Apache approached him, instead of approaching Garth, and said in a vibrant voice that carried the length of the room:

"I want to talk to you, aristocrat!"

Quickly Tomashin overcame his surprise. He decided that, doubtless, Bibi had changed the original plan; that he did not wish to force an immediate quarrel on Garth—it would be too raw, too obvious—and was going to play first an edge of comedy.

Very well. He would act up to this comedy. He was about to say something—anything . . . .

"Why . . . ." he began.

And, all at once, he was silent as, looking from Bibi

to Garth, he happened to see the wink that passed between them; as he caught a glimmer of the truth and, the next second, understood fully—understood that the plot of the carefully rehearsed drama had changed; that he himself was now cast for the rôle of victim; that, in other words, he had been double-crossed.

Yes. Double-crossed.

How . . . .? Why . . . .?

He did not know; rather, just then, had no time to figure it out.

But he was certain of it. Absolutely certain. For here was Voivenel shaking with laughter. Here was the head-waiter doubled up with gargantuan, exaggerated mirth. Here was the American thinly smiling.

Tomashin swore under his breath. He was appalled. He was furious. He was strangely indignant at the thought that, having set a trap, he himself should step into it. But he was arrogant as well as brave; and, therefore, when the Apache repeated: "I want to talk to you, aristocrat!" he rejoined:

"You *are* talking to me. In fact, you're shouting."

The crowd tittered. It stopped tittering as Bibi turned and glared at them.

Then, again, he addressed the Wallachian. He inquired by what right the blankety-blank, unmentionable specimen of a blankety-blank, unmentionable aristocrat was making sheep's eyes at Casque d'Or.

"I didn't look at her," said Tomashin.

"You raised your glass to her!"

"I did nothing of the kind."

"In other words, I'm a liar—eh . . . .?"

Once more the audience tittered. But it tittered, not at Bibi, but with him, because of his exquisite humor. Why—wasn't it amusing?—the foreigner would be in the wrong, whatever his answer. Bibi le Farceur, Bibi the Josher, had him there—had him on toast.

Nom d'un nom d'un nom de Dieu—what a superb josher—this Bibi the Josher!

Some of the tourists moved nervously. Fun was fun, and a thrill was a thrill. But this particular thrill was getting entirely too real.

They called for their bills:

"L'addition!"

"Waiter!"

"Waiter!"

The waiters paid no attention. They could not be bothered. They were having a thoroughly good time.

For Bibi le Farceur had broken into a flood of foul invective, a stream of vitriolic and memorable obscenities. He was inviting Tomashin to fight; inviting him, by the same token, to pick out his slab in the morgue right then and there . . . . "ah—*boug' de saligaud!*" he yelled, as his feline hand reached for the ever-ready dagger beneath his armpit.

And, at this moment, before Tomashin could make up his mind what to do, Malik interfered.

The Syrian was a coward. No doubt of it. But he was faithful to his one virtue, his unswerving loyalty to Tomashin. And so, while the inner man quaked with fear, the outer man acted with courage. He jumped up. He shot his fist to the Apache's jaw.

In the nick of time the latter jerked his head back; and, at once, the other gangsters came on a run, swinging chairs and bottles, while one of them, racing past Garth's table, whispered sharply:

"Quick! Behind you! The electric light!"

The American obeyed instantly. He found the switch, turned it. Evidently it controlled the lighting system of the whole place. For, immediately, the Caveau was plunged into inky blackness.

Came a confused rushing about of people in all directions. Curses. Shouts. Laughter. The grand, savage symphony of lawless men battling in the dark with a sort of passionate futility. Free-for-all fights . . . . fights for the bully sport of tickling a rib with pointed steel or smashing a nose awry with clenched fist.

Voices:

"Ah—pig!"

"You will—will you?"

"*J't'saignerei, mon p'tit loup!*"

A Cockney tourist's amazed:

"Gawd— 'e blinkin' well bit me!"

"Aughrr . . . ." a gurgling yelp of pain.

Biff! Bang!

Another cry of pain. Another English voice, a woman's, shrill, with a decided Liverpool twang:

"Oh—my necklace—help—George!"

The latter was her husband, a gentleman with faulty adenoids and buck teeth who had few equals behind the ribbon counter of Robinson, Robinson, and Robinson's Nephews, Limited. But he was not meant for heroic strife. Besides, just then, he happened to be buried beneath three roughs who smelled sickeningly of absinthe and sweat and rank tobacco and whose agile fingers, since they believed in combining business with pleasure, were exploring his pockets.

Then a thin ray of yellow stabbed through as somebody, in the struggle, kicked in the door. The noise of the tumult drifted out, into the rue des Innocents.

The policeman at the corner heard. Shrilly he blew his whistle.

At once, in the Caveau, there was a rapid swirling of bodies. Bodies half carrying and half dragging another, prone, inert body. Lugging it into the small room where Charles sat and up the back stairs.

Too, words out of the dark—now the semi-dark—in Garth's ear:

"The trick is turned! Come on!"

Quickly he followed. In passing, he spoke to Charles:

"Malik in there—don't forget . . . ."

"No, no . . . ."

And the American raced after the Apaches. He

caught up with them in a narrow alley behind the building; he piled with them into a swift Bugatti car that had been purloined less than an hour earlier; while, down the front stairs, half a dozen policemen tumbled into the Caveau, just a minute too late to stop the gangsters' flight.

Immediately afterwards Voivenel switched on the electric current. There came a dazzling, blinding flood of light; and the gendarmes advanced with drawn sabres, triumphantly showing the teeth of blue-clad, brass-buttoned authority and giving their official battle-cry:

"In the name of the law!"

They did not discover much to use the flats of their swords on nor the square toes of their stout, capable shoes—which disappointed them. Just a number of men nursing bruises and cuts. Some hysterical, unimportant tourists. Not a sign of the rowdies who had caused the riot. And, in spite of bullying questions, nobody—it was partly fear, partly loyalty—to breathe the name of Bibi le Farceur.

Then one of the policemen saw a pair of feet protruding from beneath a table. He did the logical thing: he pulled—and dragged forth a short, swarthy Syrian, unconscious, a ragged wound across his skull, and near by the beer bottle that had done it.

The police gave him first aid. Some of the onlookers—amongst them Charles de Montfort, for reasons of his own—helped. They bandaged his head; dashed cold water into his face; forced brandy between his lips.

Finally Malik came out of his daze. His first concern was for Prince Tomashin. He looked; did not see him; saw, on the floor, Tomashin's crushed hat and broken walkingstick—mute evidence of his struggle.

Malik staggered to his feet. Anxiously, excitedly, he turned to the police. He was about to complain to them, to tell them of the attack.

But, right then, Charles, the good Samaritan who had given him the brandy, whispered to him:

"Not a word—or Tomashin's life isn't worth a centime!"

Malik obeyed.

"Don't trouble about me," he said to the sergeant who, pencil and pad in hand, was speaking pompously of taking down Monsieur's evidence and deposition. "I came here alone—a bit drunk . . . ."

"But what happened, Monsieur?"

"I got into a fight."

"With whom?"

"I don't know. Entirely my own fault. Anyway, no harm done except a headache . . . ."

Sergeant Leroux shrugged his massive shoulders. He grumbled—although, in sober fact, he felt immensely relieved about the outcome of the affair; was glad that no names had been mentioned and no accusations made. For he had been the last to arrive on the scene of battle; had run past the dark alley in back of the Caveau where the Bugatti car had been drawn up; and was practically certain that he had recognized Bibi le Farceur amongst the gangsters who had piled into the automobile, carrying an unconscious man—doubtless a wounded comrade—between them.

And—to arrest this Bibi, this ruthless, red-handed assassin . . . .? Why—Sergeant Leroux was a married man, with three small children . . . .

Therefore he decided to leave well enough alone; and, after a stern if hypocritical word of admonition to the crowd to mind their *p's* and *q's* in the future, he led the gendarmes out of the restaurant.

The tourists followed, still frightened and excited. Presently only a handful of people was left; half a dozen roughs; a few cheap cocottes; Charles de Montfort, sitting in a corner and talking to Malik in a low, confidential voice; and one solitary, middle-aged, red-faced Briton.

The latter had remained serene and rather bored throughout the commotion; and, being the sort of Englishman who believed that alcohol is food and that whiskey well shaken in a cocktail contains valuable calories, he turned now to one of the waiters.

"Another one," he hiccoughed in execrable French. "Same as before, Alphonse."

For he called all French waiters Alphonse and all German waiters Hans. He considered this the height of smart, cosmopolitan humor.

Not that Mr. Breckinridge Jones—such was his name—was stupid.

On the contrary. He was an exceedingly clever man, at least in business matters, and made a good living in the City of London.

A very good living. Vintage champagne with and between his meals. Charming service-flat in Mayfair. Apartment in Paris. Expensive wife. Expensive mistress. Rolls-Royce limousine and Bentley roadster. Shooting box in Scotland. Trout stream in Norway.

Just mention his name to any City man of your acquaintance. And if the City man does not recollect immediately, mention the Great Danish Health-Bread Syndicate; or the Orange-Cure-Dyspepsia Sanitarium; or the High and Mighty Lodge of True-Blue All-British Knights.

You'll hear things. Perhaps you'll be offered, very cheaply, gorgeously engraved stock and bond certificates in these three concerns.

Don't buy. Rather buy Brooklyn Bridge.

Oh yes. Mr. Breckinridge Jones was an exceedingly clever man.

Too, he was lucky. He was, furthermore, a reckless gambler. And—following an "inside" market tip given him by an old friend, a Chicago newspaper correspondent, the same to whom Garth Brent had been listening, late this afternoon, at the Ritz bar—he had been forcing his gambler's luck. For he had plunged heavily at the Paris *bourse*, buying huge blocks of munition shares and short-selling Wallachian government securities; convinced that, a week from Saturday, Danielo would enter the capital of his native land and claim the throne, that there would be revolution and war—and, of course, profits.

He was thinking of these profits now. He was debating, in a rather maudlin way, whether he should buy the pearl necklace for his wife and the emerald dog-collar for his mistress or the other way around.

He could not overhear the conversation between the two men—Malik and Charles de Montfort—at a nearby table. He was not, therefore, able to guess ahead of time what was destined to happen twenty-four hours later: namely, that Danielo would not claim the throne—that the republic would continue—that there would be no strife—that, in consequence, munition shares would drop amazingly while Wallachian securities would rise—and that, in further consequence, he himself, like so many other speculators, would have to file a petition in bankruptcy.

Only a few words he overheard.

"Malik," Charles was saying, "it's no use trying to argue."

But these words meant nothing to Mr. Jones—though they meant a great deal to Malik, causing him to stare with hate and despair at Charles who added:

"You play poker?"

"A little. Why?"

"Because we, my friend Garth Brent and I, hold four aces—not to forget the joker. A joker called Tomashin. This gentleman—if you will pardon my melodramatic way of putting it—is absolutely in our power."

"I know," mumbled the Syrian.

Tomashin—he thought—the one human being whom he loved, to whom he was devoted, and—yes! —in the power of the American, the power of Bibi; Bibi who had double-crossed him and who, as the smiling Frenchman pointed out a moment later, was decidedly careless when it came to taking human life, provided he be urged on by sufficient passion—or sufficient pay.

Again, with hate and despair, he stared at the other. His lower lip sagged; the upper curled into a stark grimace. Unhuman—he seemed to Charles who, almost, felt sorry—like a figure in some terrible, grotesque wax-work.

"What do you want me to do?" he forced out the question with physical effort.

"I offer you a trade."

"A trade . . . .?"

"We shall turn over to you, a week from next Saturday, your beloved Tomashin, unharmed—while you, within the hour, will turn over to us La Sylphe. Understood?"

"Yes," said the Syrian.

He shrugged his shoulders. He hated this smiling

Frenchman; hated the American; would always hate them. Still, he was an Oriental, thus a man who, brazenly practical, knew when he was beaten, who would go to the end of a bad situation in his fatalistic way without squirming, and wasting neither thought nor tissue on something which destiny had written.

"Yes," he repeated.

"Very well. And—one more condition . . . ."

"What is it?"

"You will tell us the whereabouts of Prince Danielo."

And then, suddenly, Malik broke into laughter; hysterical laughter . . . . "laughter," Charles described it later on to Garth, "that fell like a blight—laughter that frightened me—laughter as if at a joke hatched in hell . . . ."

The Frenchman leaned forward. He gripped Malik's shoulder and shook him.

"What's the matter?" he demanded.

Once more the Syrian laughed; stammered out, choking, gurgling, strangling with bitter mirth:

"Danielo's whereabouts . . . .? His whereabouts—eh? Ah—a grave—a quiet, silent grave—that's his whereabouts . . . ."

And then, when Charles was speechless with utter amazement, the other continued:

"Might as well tell you—since the game is over and you're bound to find out sooner or later. You see—Danielo died—he died six months ago . . . ."

CHAPTER ELEVEN

GARTH BRENT never forgot that wild ride through the night. Often, in the years to come, he would speak of it—the stolen Bugatti car; Bibi le Farceur at the wheel, driving at reckless, lawless speed; the other gangsters piled in pellmell; and, at the bottom of the tonneau, securely bound and gagged though no longer unconscious, Prince Tomashin.

"Staring up at me he was," the American would say. "Staring up at me—not with hate. Hate I wouldn't have minded. An honest emotion—hate—which I returned fully. But there was an expression in his eyes like—oh—like that of a slaughtered soul—as if, in his heart, the last faith had died, the last hope. And I—well—I couldn't stand it . . . ."

So Garth looked away from those staring eyes. He looked, instead, at the houses that heaved on either side of the speeding automobile like things that were alive and breathing, at the street lamps swaying like yellow banners carried in a parade; while, ever farther into the distance, dropped the Paris which he knew best, the gay, laughing, patchouli-scented, champagne-popping Paris of the foreigners, wasting daily the dollars hard earned in New York, Buenos Aires, London, Shanghai, Valparaiso; and while ever nearer came the other Paris, the grim Paris that stood tall and black beneath the tall, black sky.

Finally they reached the rue des Gobelins where, in a small garage, they stabled the Bugatti. Then, a revolver pressed persuasively against Tomashin's side, they descended a steep flight of rickety, wooden steps that led down to the river.

Not the Seine. But a river, quite unknown to Anglo-Saxon tourists, that was called the Bièvre; that bloated rather than rolled along; that was semi-liquid and of a dark chocolate color; that crawled onward like a sluggish beast, turgid and viscous and stinking, most fitly emptying its nauseous waters—and perhaps once in a while a corpse with glazed eyes and knife stuck between shoulder blades—into the immense central sewer, together with the rest of the Paris refuse.

A gloomy, melancholy spot . . . . and Garth grew depressed as he followed the Apaches into the heart of the ancient quarter—and the wind there howled like a starving wolf, and the blackness there was blacker than ink, and how the gangsters found their way, except by smell, was more than the American could guess.

So black it was that he was able to see neither house nor man nor beast; at least, but dimly saw—like blurred, wiped-over, ebony silhouettes against a background of yet deeper ebony. But life was everywhere.

Everywhere he was maddeningly conscious of eyes staring at him through the darkness, used to that same darkness. Occasionally he heard the Apaches speak with people he could not see in a metallic slang he could not understand; heard feet pattering away on incredible and mysterious errands; heard the shiver of garments brushing past; heard a girl's tinkling, high laughter; heard the clashing of cheap, tinny jewelry.

Once, coming out of that inky void with stark distinctness, he heard a cry; a cry of infinite fear and desolation. Then a heavy thud; a rattling, agonized gurgle as if deep from a man's throat—or, perhaps, a woman's.

Then silence. No sign anywhere. No twinkle of killing dagger stabbing the opaque. No actual, physical sight to motivate, to explain. Just the cry—the thud—the death gurgle—and the silence. One of those cruel, sardonic Paris mysteries that baffle probability. Like the loose ends of a tragic tale with no climax—thought Garth—like the words of a grim jest without a point . . . .

And he shivered; and, had he been a Catholic, he would have crossed himself and doubtless felt the better for it; and he gave a sigh of relief when, a few moments later, he saw the misty outlines of a house and when Bibi said to him:

"Here we are. My baronial estate—at your service."

He led the way into a dimly lit hall with two doors. He added:

"I suppose M. de Montfort told you about the two dirty tricks which this specimen of an unmentionable aristocrat," pointing at Tomashin, "hired me to pull off?"

"Yes," smiled Garth. "The first trick was to kidnap me. And the second . . . .?"

"The second," interrupted Bibi with a laugh, "is in the next room. A surprise for you, citizen. A present—with my compliments!"

He opened the left door. He closed it again, after having pushed Garth across the threshold; and the latter stood there; and, because of the swathing blackness of the streets, the light blinded him momentarily; and he blinked his eyes; and then he heard a voice:

"Garth—oh Garth Brent—I have been waiting for you—praying for you. For I needed your help—oh—I needed you so . . . ."

And then, blinking his last blink, he saw La Sylphe.

He should have been utterly astonished.

He should have—would have—exclaimed, had he been an every-day, prosy, painfully normal young man:

"Good heavens! How did *you* get here?"

Or, changing the intonation:

"Good heavens! How did you *get* here?"

Or, again changing the intonation:

"Good heavens! How did you get *here?*"

But then he knew how she had got there. Bibi had as good as told him. Besides, he was not an everyday, prosy, painfully normal young man; and here was a situation which appealed to all his romantic instincts: a Princess—kidnapped; a Princess whom, like a hero in a fairy tale, he had rescued . . . .

And so he walked over to her. He bowed very deeply. He kissed her left hand and then her right; and he said:

"I'm sure this is a dream—such a wonderful, glorious dream."

"Why do you think so?" she asked in a low voice.

"Because how—except in a dream—would I dare tell you that never have I seen such lips as yours? Ah—slender, red lips of kisses! And how—except in a dream—would I dare . . . .?"

He was silent; and she demanded:

"Would you dare—what?"

"This!"

He took her in his arms; he pressed his mouth to hers; and, in that queer, picaresque, amazingly un-American way of his, he went on:

"There is a song for you in my heart. I know the verses—but I cannot speak them. My soul is humming the very tune—but I cannot sing it. My love—you see—my love is so great it chokes me . . . ."

She smiled.

"My dear," she said, "I used to think of you as a bold man—such a bold, reckless American—the sort one reads about in books. And now—I'm afraid I know you to be . . . ."

"What?"

"A poet."

"Can't I be both poet and bold, reckless man? Did not the troubadours fight as well as rhyme? Can't I carry a lute in my left hand—a sword in my right hand . . . .?"

"Never mind the sword. Tell me how much you love me."

So he told her.

He told her mad things, tender things. He told her how, in this world of flying passions and fading lusts, she was his one true love. He told her that his love for her was a garden sweeter than Eden and a town prouder than Rome. And, being the kind of man he was, he went on in this strain for quite a while; and, still being the kind of man he was, he added, with a sudden shift of speech:

"I do hope you like breakfast in bed. I adore it—chiefly on Sundays."

"Breakfast in bed . . . .?" she echoed.

"I mean—for two."

She laughed.

"Why—" she exclaimed—"this is either a proposal of marriage—or else . . . ."

"No 'or else' about it," he cut in hurriedly. "Will you be my wife?"

"Yes."

Again she laughed. She continued:

"So strange!"

"How so?"

"We've known each other only twenty-four hours."

"Wrong, darling. We've known each other a lifetime—and more than a mere lifetime. For I have always known you, dear. I have always loved you—in this life—and all my past lives . . . ."

He slurred; paused; demanded:

"And—*you*. . . . .?"

"I have always known *you*—I always loved *you* . . . ."

Once more he kissed her. Rather, it was she who kissed him. With an almost brutal movement of her head, she tilted up her face and caught his lips to hers.

She looked at him through half-closed lids. She smiled. She said:

"I like your necktie."

"I'm glad you like it."

"And I like the way the hair curls on your temples."

"Oh—don't be silly!"

"I'm not silly. I'm sensible."

Then there were questions she asked. Quite a few. For instance:

"Why do you love me?"

"When did you first love me?"

"Will you always love me?"

Aspiring questions. Questions quite impossible to answer. But Garth did his best; and heaven knows what other sentimental foolishness he would have whispered to her if not, a few moments later, the door had opened to admit Charles de Montfort.

The latter was excited. He said, when introductions had been made and he had bowed over La Sylphe's hand:

"I brought Malik. I had a talk with him . . . ."

"And . . . .?"

The Frenchman hesitated.

"I—" he went on, addressing the girl—"I'm afraid I have sad news . . . ."

"Yes," she interrupted him. "About my brother Danielo . . . ."

"You—you know . . . .?"

"I do." She turned to Garth. "Danielo died—half a year ago . . . ."

The American was amazed.

"Oh—" he cried.

Then she explained; explained all that had happened to her.

This afternoon she had received a telegram signed by Karolus. Faked. Of course. But she had not guessed it at the time. So—exactly as Doderet, the stage door man at the Ambassadeurs had described to Garth—she had left the theatre to hurry to the station and catch the Lyons train, and a taxicab had driven up. She had jumped in; had felt, at once, strong arms about her; and, before she could make an outcry, a sponge soaked in chloroform had been pressed to her nostrils.

When she had regained consciousness she had found herself in this room. Tomashin had stood over her. He had put all his cards on the table.

First he had told her of Danielo's death.

It seemed that he had died in Budapest; and the news had been kept secret, completely and successfully, by the royalists. For they had understood that, to broadcast the event, would have meant an end to their plans, since, with Mussolini now unable to fulfil his promise of a marriage between Danielo and Princess Maria di Savoia, daughter of the King of Italy, that country no longer would have a plausible reason to throw in its influence in favor of the former dynasty and against the republic supported by France. The intention—Tomashin had added—had been to hush up the tragic tidings until a week from Saturday, the date of Danielo's coming of age, had he been alive.

"But why . . . .?" the girl had demanded.

"Because you, Nadine," he had replied, "are Danielo's twin-sister. Because, now that Danielo is in his grave, you are the rightful claimant to the throne. Because, furthermore, in your possession, hidden by the top seam of your veil, is the ancient, iron crown . . . ."

"Still—I do not see . . . ."

"Don't you? Listen. A week from Saturday you

will enter the capital of Wallachia. You will declare yourself Queen. But you will not rule alone. For, according to the law of our land, if a woman inherits the throne she must share it with the man she marries . . . ."

"The man I marry . . . .?" she had stammered.

She had guessed the answer; and it had come:

"Myself!"

Then, when, in fear, in anger, in indignation, she had exclaimed that never, never, never would she be his, he had continued:

"You remember Protopieff, the Archimandrate, the high-priest of our Holy Orthodox Church . . . .?"

"Yes."

"He, too, is a royalist and in exile. He will be here before the morning to make us man and wife."

"You—oh—you would not force me to . . . .? You would not dare . . . ."

"I would dare—anything. For love of you? No—though I do love you, Nadine. But for the sake of my ambition—my love of Wallachia—my hate of the republic . . . ."

She had tried to reason with him; and he had turned on her sternly:

"Be quiet. It's useless to argue. My mind is made up. Tonight we marry. You will remain here a day or two. Then—all this has been arranged—a swift car will take us across Europe to our own country."

There had been a pause.

"Ah—" he had gone on; and he had been like a man exalted—"our own country again, from sea to sea and from mountain to mountain. Our own country—happy again and prosperous and blessed by all the dear Saints—with you and me to guard its destinies. Oh—" he had cried impatiently, when she had not replied—"does not the thought of it stir you—the thought of our glory and pride and high station—the thought of throne and sceptre—of a grand epic come true . . . .?"

When still she had been silent, he had shrugged his shoulders.

"This thing has been decided," he had said. "A week from Saturday—you and I—side by side—on the throne. And—" with a hard, chilly threat—"if you disobey or rebel—remember—there was once a man, your late father's twin-brother, who disobeyed—who was imprisoned in a monastery. Convents, too, have walls—high walls . . . ."

Vividly the girl described the scene—and Garth was conscious of a queer, illogical feeling of admiration for Prince Tomashin. One of those medieval aristocrats—he considered him—whose cold, sincere arrogance was steel rather than iron and diamond rather than steel; one of those Machiavellian conspirators whose weapon was the sword rather than the pistol and the dagger rather than the sword. Yet a brave man; and, in his own way, an honest patriot . . . .

The next moment, Garth's thoughts were interrupted by a violent commotion that drifted through the door from the entrance hall.

There was Bibi le Farceur's strident voice, shouting rich, metallic, and obscene slang. There was another voice, speaking in French though with a heavy, foreign accent, demanding furiously:

"What—what do you mean by this . . . .?"

"I mean," replied Bibi, "that—how shall I put it and respect your saintly calling?—ah—I have it—I mean that you have put your ugly nose and both your ugly flat feet into the soup—you understand—*hein* . . . . ?"

"This is an outrage!"

"If you don't stop yelling, I'll be obliged to slit your scrawny gullet from ear to ear!"

Garth flung open the door.

He saw, surrounded by the amused gangsters, a tall man dressed in sombre, clerical black; a man—to judge by his face—as much a medieval, Gothic fanatic as Tomashin; a divine who believed more in the God of wrath than in the Virgin Mary whom the God of love kissed in Galilee. Protopieff—doubtless—the Archimandrate of the Orthodox Wallachian Church, here to make Tomashin and La Sylphe man and wife . . . .

And a notion popped into the American's head. He whispered to the girl; she whispered back: "Yes;" and he stepped up to Protopieff and said:

"You've come to perform a wedding ceremony—haven't you? Well—the bride is still willing. But the bridegroom has changed his mind."

"Eh . . . .?"

"Another man will take his place, Your Reverence."

"*Nom d'un nom d'un nom de Dieu!*" exclaimed Bibi, roaring with laughter. "An idea worthy of myself!"

So, presently, there was this fantastic and incongruous scene—here, in the heart of the Paris Apache quarter. A romantic young man leading to the altar—not much of an altar, in fact no more than a scarred, spotted pine table covered with glasses and bottles and cigarette butts and some tattered copies of *Le Petit Parisien*—a Princess of the blood; and, for witnesses, a French nobleman and half a dozen gangsters who—to tell a regrettable truth—were using quite shocking threats to force a lean ecclesiastic to pronounce the ritual phrase:

". . . . and whom God hath joined together, let no man put asunder . . . . Amen . . . ."

Harshly he uttered the words; inimically. And then, suddenly—perhaps because he saw the great love in Garth's eyes and La Sylphe's; perhaps because, at the last, the sacredness of the occasion spoke to his priestly soul—he raised his arms in blessing and continued in a softer voice:

"*Copula, felices ter et amplius, quos irrupta tenet!*"

Thus they became man and wife; and Charles de Montfort and Bibi le Farceur—indeed why shouldn't they?—kissed the bride; and, a few minutes later, Garth went to the next room and cut Tomashin's bonds and said:

"You are free to go."

He stretched out a hand. He was, after all, an American, therefore a sentimentalist, bearing no grudge against a defeated foe.

But Tomashin was a man of a different breed.

"I have lost," he replied. "I have lost—" and he spoke without the slightest theatricality—"a kingdom —thanks to you. You are my enemy. Why should I shake hands with you . . . .?"

And he bowed with icy politeness; he left, followed by Protopieff and Malik, while Garth rejoined the others—and laughed as he saw the wedding breakfast that was being prepared by one of the Apaches: an omelette as light as a feather, salad with a rich dressing that had just a suspicion of onion juice, crisp, wheaten bread, and a couple of bottles of red wine that were not bad at all.

Perhaps the coffee was too weak.

However . . . .

A jolly, gay little meal it was, with young day booming up on the horizon and, presently, the sun rays beginning to dance in through the window and painting the room with orange high-lights and delicate, heliotrope shadows, and, outside, somebody not very sober singing:

> *"Depis, c'est moi qu'est l'sout'neur*
> *Naturel à ma p'tit' soeur,*
> *Qu'est l'ami' d'la p'tit' Cécile*
> *A Bell'ville . . . ."*

It was quite typical that the gangsters should be the most correct in the use of knife and fork and the most exorbitantly polite—at least as they understood politeness. Thus Bibi le Farceur assured La Sylphe that, in the past, he had been a fanatic radical, despising all aristocrats and hating all Kings and Queens; that he would have thought no more of croaking a crowned head, male or female, than he would of gutting a mackerel; but that after one look into her eyes . . . . he rose; he raised his glass; he exclaimed:

"Down with the French republic! Hereafter I am a royalist! And, in the coming election, I shall spit on the Tricolor and vote for the pretender, the Bourbon, His Highness the Duke of Orleans!"

Then, when La Sylphe had gone to the next room to sit in front of a cracked mirror and do this and that to her hair, Garth and Charles were having a confidential talk.

"Where will you spend your honeymoon?" asked the latter. "At the Riviera . . . .?"

"At the Riviera . . . .? Amongst the London

stock-brokers with diamond studs in their evening dress shirts? Amongst the Germans wearing Jaeger woollens and peacock feathers on their green Tyrolese hats? Amongst my own countrymen calling plaintively for cocktails before breakfast? Amongst the gigolos and pansies and cocottes of all nations? Not I! I am now a respectable married man. Besides," he added, with a yawn, "the Riviera is too far away—and I'm tired—so tired. You know—I've been on my feet, almost continuously, for two nights and a day . . . ."

"Well—you must go somewhere . . . ."

"What's wrong with my pleasant little rooms at Marly-le-Roi?"

"Ghosts."

"Ghosts . . . .?"

"The blond ghost of Ninon—the brunette ghost of charming Suzette . . . ."

"Oh—I've forgotten them. Once more—" and, queerly, in spite of his flippant language, the American meant it—"I am simon-pure, pristine, almost virginal."

He paused; went on:

"Still—that reminds me—do something for me, will you . . . .?"

"Of course. What is it?"

"Telephone to my faithful but tactless dinge. You see—if I appear this time of day with La Sylphe, George is bound to imagine the worst—and the chances are he'll pull one of his dirty African-Baptist wise-cracks . . . ."

"I'll explain to him," laughed the other.

"And explain to your mother, too. You might tell her, incidentally, that I'm taking her tip."

"Which one?"

"Honest work for me in the future. I've got me a job."

"With whom?"

"With my uncle."

"Uncle Cornelius—back in America?"

"No. With my new uncle—though he doesn't know it yet."

"Whom do you mean?"

"My uncle by marriage. Sir Pascal. I've decided to be his private secretary—instead of Dennis Courvoisier who'll get the air. And, first thing out of the box, I'll do my best to find out how he made his gigantic fortune . . . ."

"And, I suppose," came the ironic question, "being an American, you'll try and do likewise . . . ?"

"Precisely. I am—as you say—an American. I am not—as someone I don't care to mention by name—a rakish, loose-living, skirt-chasing French bachelor. Furthermore, I have my future children to think of . . . ."

Charles burst into a roar of laughter.

"Farewell, romance!" he exclaimed, throwing up

his hands. "Welcome, flannel underwear—and perambulators—and rubber nipples—and . . . ."

"Oh—shut up!"

A few minutes later, Garth and La Sylphe left the house and went in the direction of the rue des Gobelins where, in the small garage, next to the stolen Bugatti, Charles had parked the American's roadster.

Morning had come. Blue-and-rose morning of Spring—brushing into the ancient quarter on quivering, gauzy wings; hovering birdlike over the sordid, tarred rooftops; dropping liquid silver over the mazed, scabbed streets; adding music to the strident calls of pavement and gutter; gilding the dirt and murk of the bloated, evil river—the Bièvre—along whose banks they walked, hand in hand.

They reached the rickety, wooden steps that led up to the rue des Gobelins. There Garth stopped. He turned to La Sylphe.

"Will you give me a wedding present?" he asked.

"Gladly."

"A very special one . . . ."

"What is it, dear?"

"The iron crown of Wallachia . . . ."

"The—oh—the iron crown . . . .?" she echoed.

"Yes."

"But—what for . . . .?"

"To do with as I please."

She hesitated. Perhaps she read what was in his

mind. Then she slipped it from the top seam of her veil and gave it to him.

He looked at it.

A narrow, flexible metal band, exquisitely chiseled and carved. A symbol—he thought—that, throughout the gray, swinging centuries—had seen history and made history. A symbol for whose sake men had been slaughtered and widows and orphans had wept. A symbol above which had blown and blustered the intolerant trumpets of pride and honor. A symbol dark and grim and forbidding. A symbol that, today, was overshadowed by the wild, white cross of freedom . . . .

And, suddenly, Garth curved his right arm. He threw with skill and strength, as he might throw a baseball—and the iron crown of Wallachia dropped into the Bièvre—was swirled away in a whirlpool of brown dirt—and gurgled out of sight, very innocuous and very harmless.

Then he turned again to La Sylphe.

"My dear," he said, being still a romantic young man, "only a fool would call your hair red. The color of autumn leaves it is—with a memory of pure gold . . . ."

And then, careless of who might be watching, he kissed her . . . .

www.ingramcontent.com/pod-product-compliance
Lightning Source LLC
Chambersburg PA
CBHW030342310726
48979CB00001B/147

* 9 7 8 1 4 3 4 4 9 9 4 1 7 *